FAMILY TIME

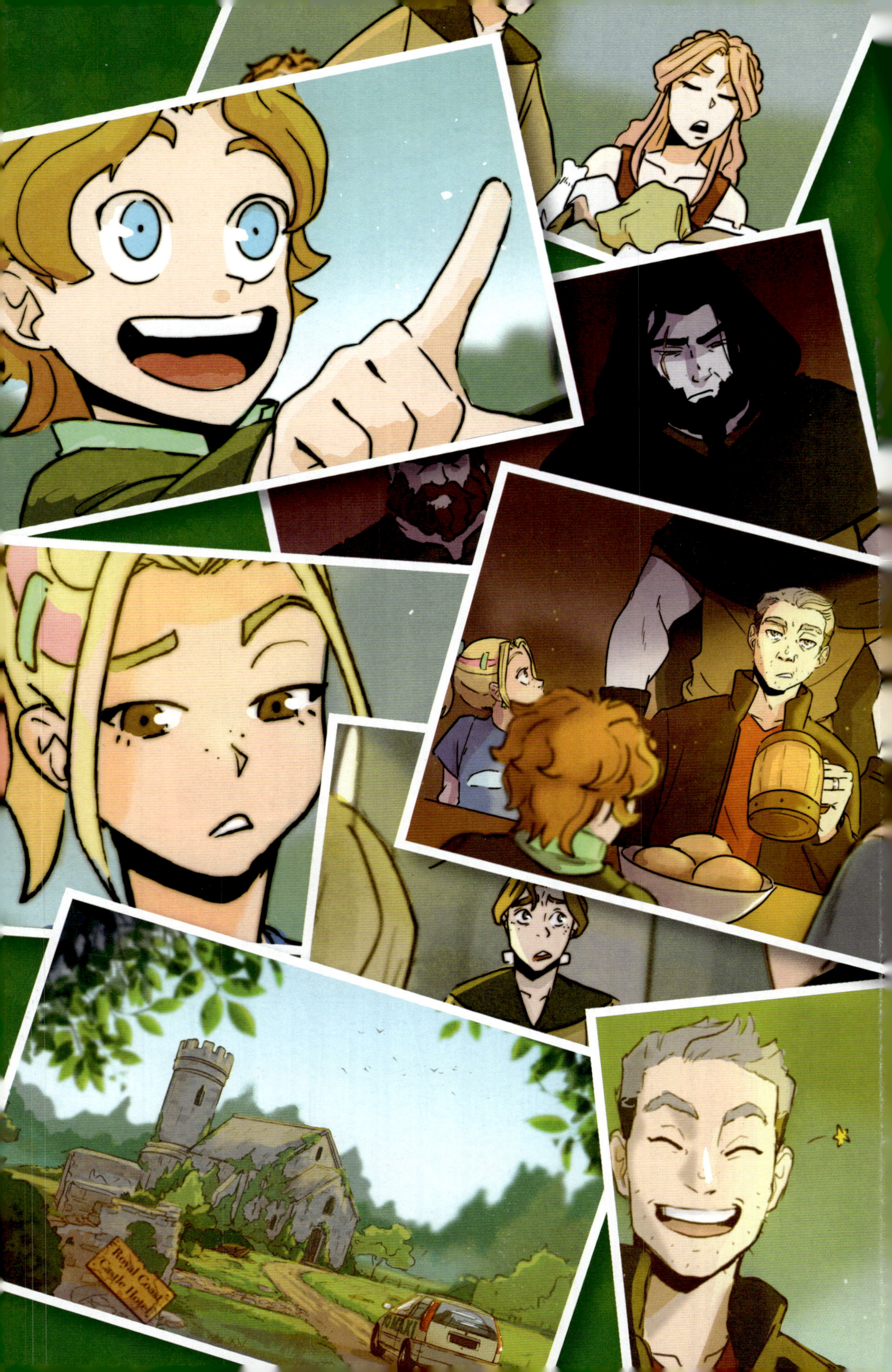
Royal Coast Castle Hotel

FAMILY TIME

WRITERS
LILY WINDOM & ROBERT WINDOM

ARTIST
ASIAH FULMORE

LETTERS
CRANK! (#2-4)
& SIMON BOWLAND (#1)

LOGO DESIGN
SERBAN CRISTESCU

CAB LICENSE
RORY CONALL

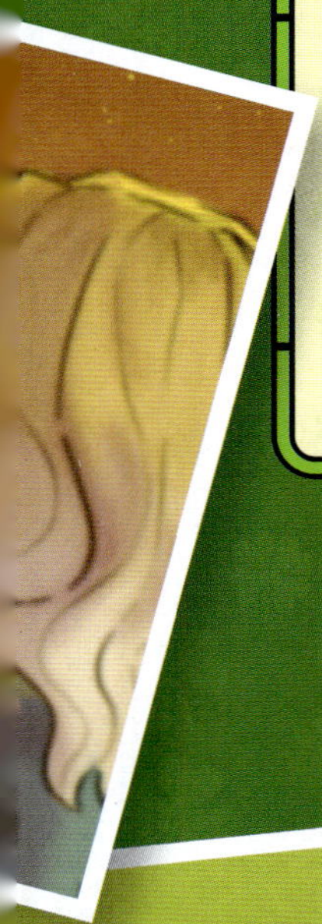

White Plains Public Library, White Plains, NY

FOR ABLAZE
MANAGING EDITOR
RICH YOUNG
EDITOR
KEVIN KETNER
ASSOCIATE EDITOR
AMY JACKSON
DESIGNERS
RODOLFO MURAGUCHI
& **JULIA STEZOVSKY**

Publisher's Cataloging-in-Publication data

Names: Windom, Lily, author. | Windom, Robert, author. | Fulmore, Asiah, artist. Title: Family time / by Lily Windom and Robert Windom; art by Asiah Fulmore. Description: Portland, OR: Ablaze. Identifiers: ISBN: 978-1-68497-132-9 Subjects: LCSH Time travel—Comic books, strips, etc. | Time travel—Juvenile fiction. | Ireland—History—Comic books, strips, etc. | Ireland—History—Juvenile fiction. | Fantasy comic books, strips, etc. | Graphic novels. | BISAC JUVENILE FICTION / Comics & Graphic Novels / Fantasy | COMICS & GRAPHIC NOVELS / Fantasy | COMICS & GRAPHIC NOVELS / Historical fiction. Classification: LCC PZ7.1 .W56 Fa 2023 | DDC 741.5—dc23

/ABLAZEPUB
@ABLAZEPUB
@ABLAZEPUB
WWW.ABLAZE.NET

FAMILY TIME. Published by Ablaze Publishing, 11222 SE Main St. #22906 Portland, OR 97269. Family Time © 2022 Robert Windom. Ablaze TM & © 2022 ABLAZE, LLC. All rights reserved. Ablaze TM & © 2023 ABLAZE, LLC. All rights reserved. Ablaze and its logo TM & © 2023 Ablaze, LLC. All Rights Reserved. All names, characters, events, and locales in this publication are entirely fictional. Any resemblance to actual persons (living or dead), events or places, without satiric intent is coincidental. No portion of this book may be reproduced by any means (digital or print) without the written permission of Ablaze Publishing except for review purposes. Printed in China. This book may be purchased for educational, business, or promotional use in bulk. For sales information, advertising opportunities and licensing email:info@ablazepublishing.com

10 9 8 7 6 5 4 3 2 1

#1 MAIN COVER BY **JAE LEE**

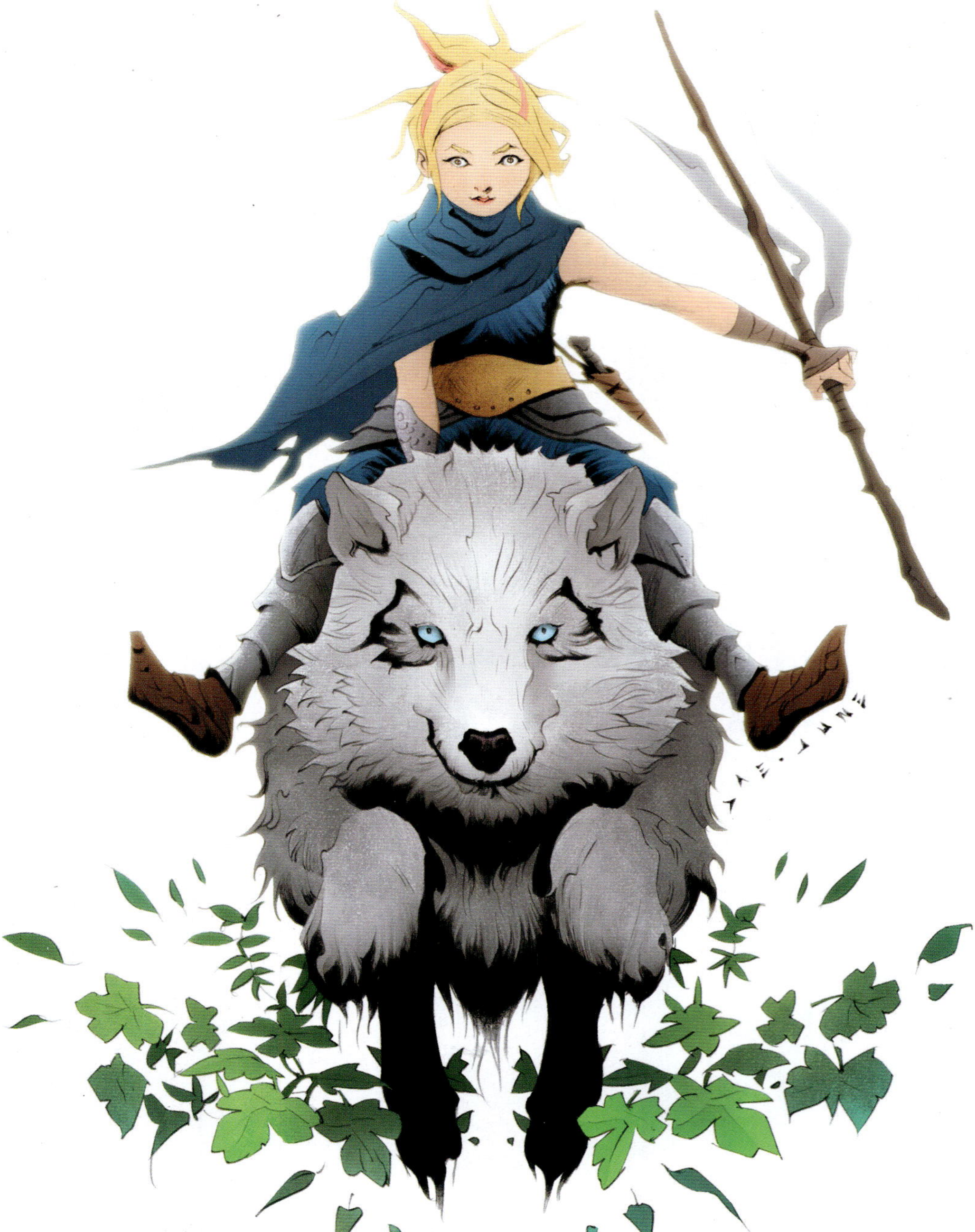

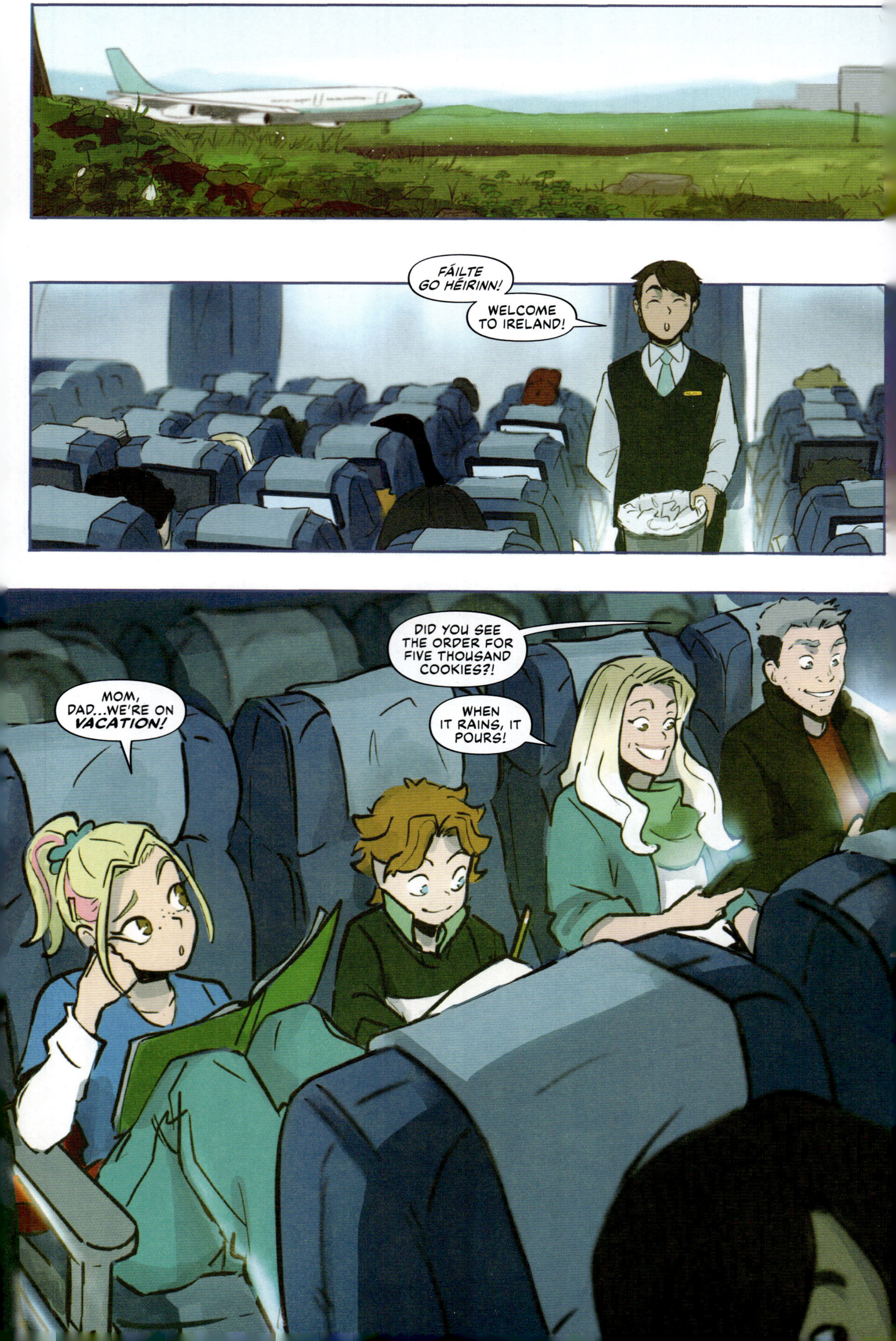
FÁILTE GO HÉIRINN!
WELCOME TO IRELAND!
MOM, DAD...WE'RE ON *VACATION!*
DID YOU SEE THE ORDER FOR FIVE THOUSAND COOKIES?!
WHEN IT RAINS, IT POURS!

O'CONNELL FAMILY COOKIES ARE *MELTIN'*, BOO!
HISTORICAL REENACTMENTS: The New Travel Rage
Through the Ages
THAT DIDN'T DESERVE A HIGH FIVE.
Puzzle
JEEZ... THIS IS HEAVY, KIDS!

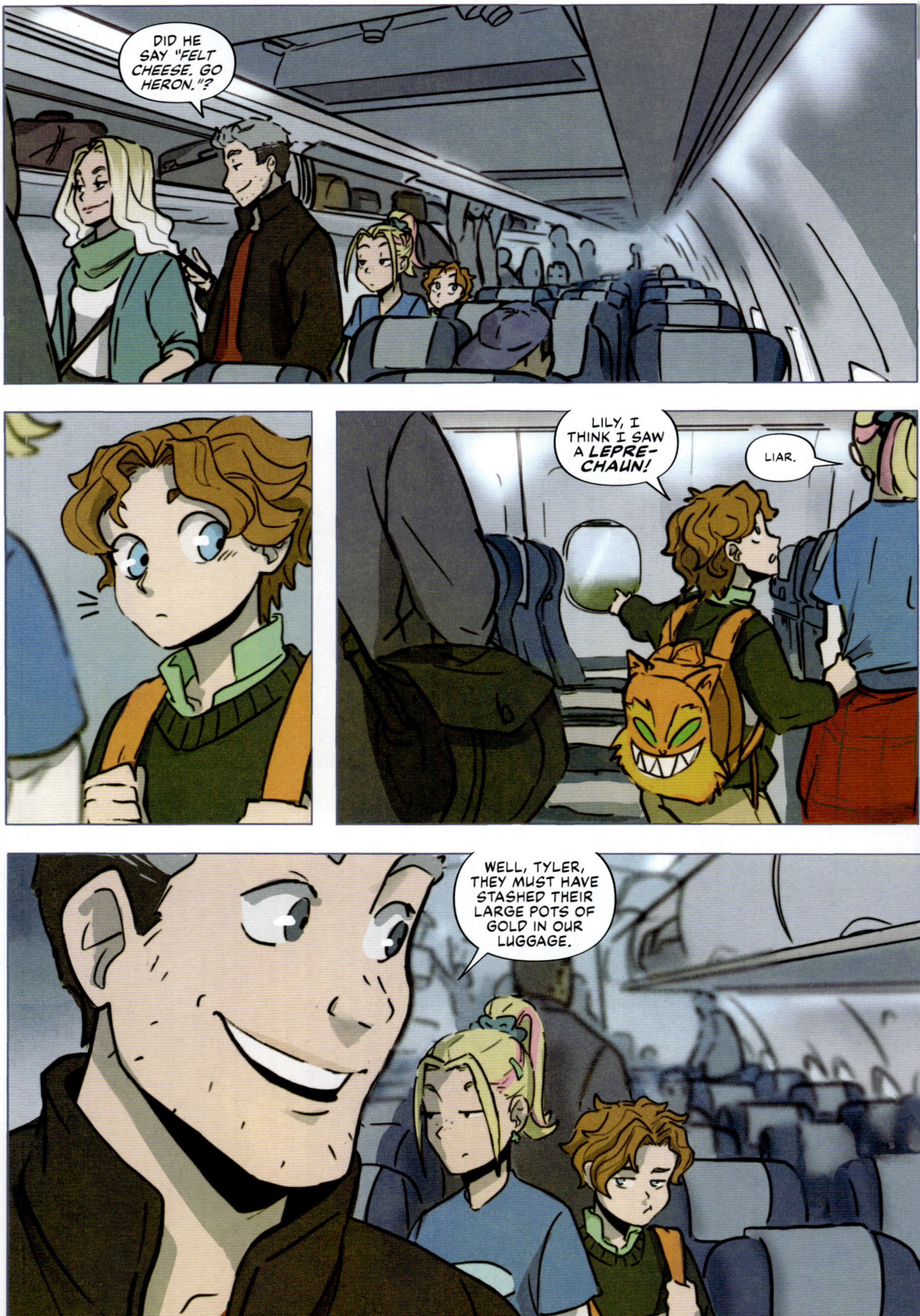
DID HE SAY "FELT CHEESE. GO HERON."?
LILY, I THINK I SAW A LEPRE-CHAUN!
LIAR.
WELL, TYLER, THEY MUST HAVE STASHED THEIR LARGE POTS OF GOLD IN OUR LUGGAGE.

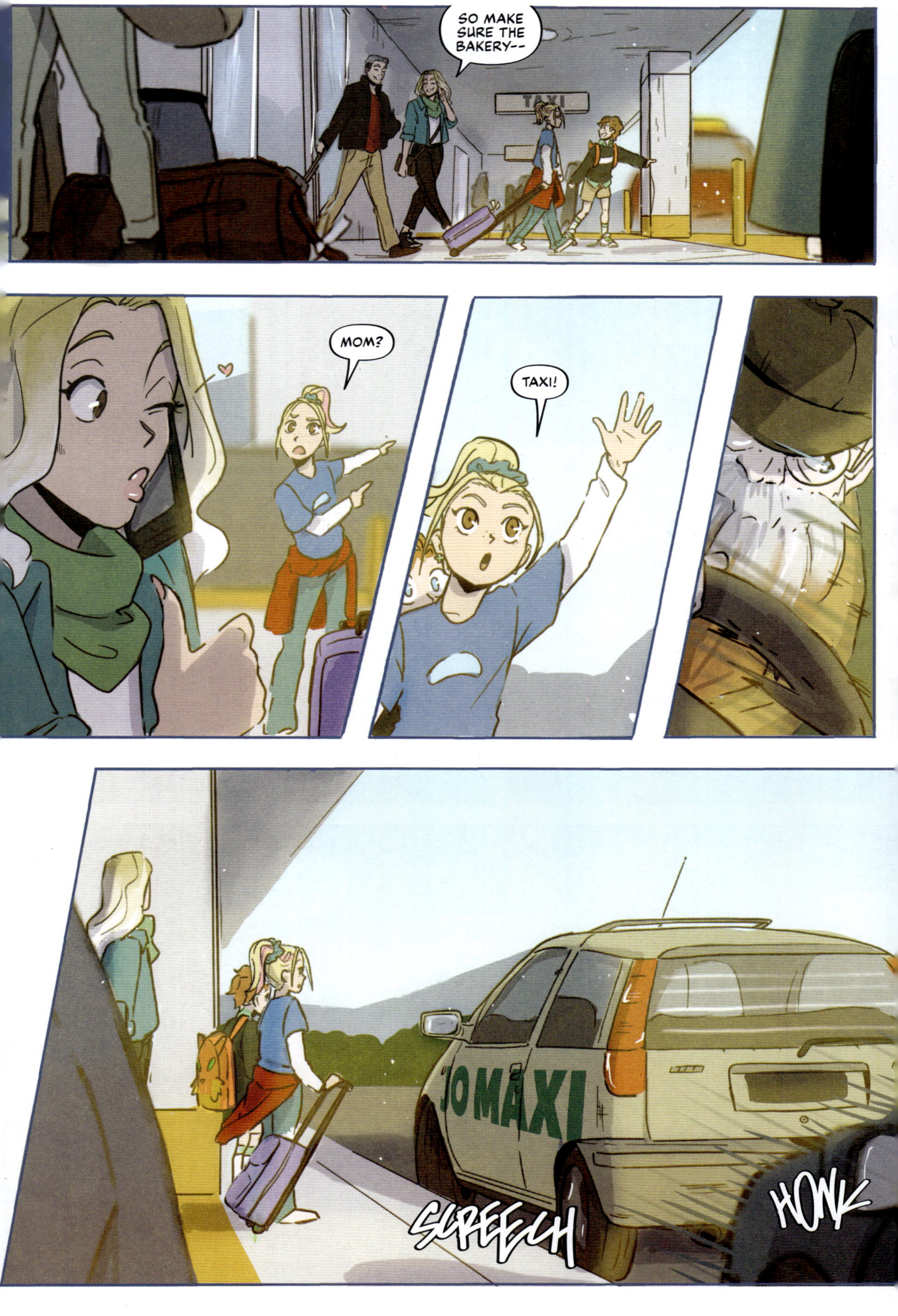
SO MAKE SURE THE BAKERY--
TAXI
MOM?
TAXI!
JOMAXI
SCREECH
HONK

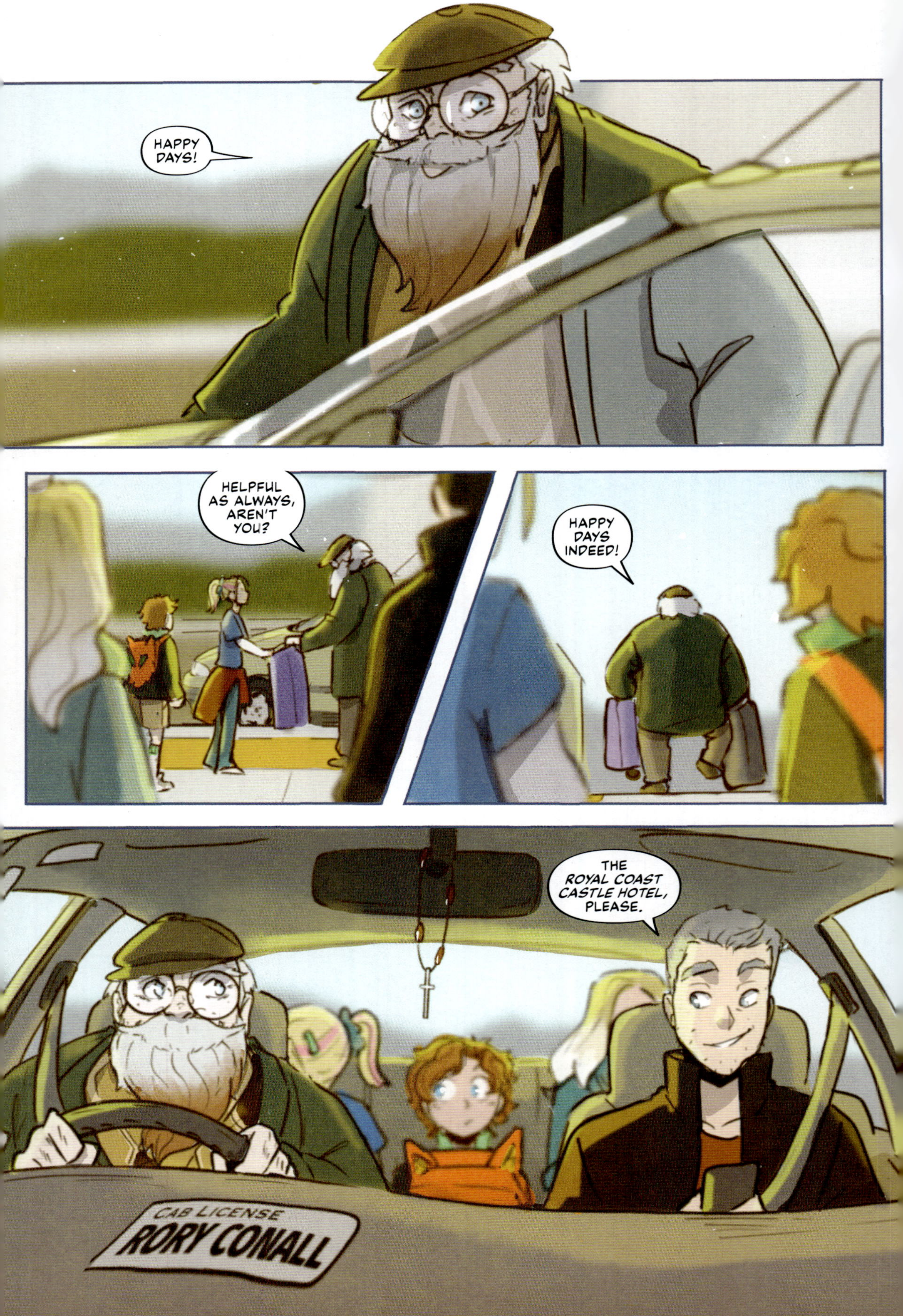
HAPPY DAYS!
HELPFUL AS ALWAYS, AREN'T YOU?
HAPPY DAYS INDEED!
THE ROYAL COAST CASTLE HOTEL, PLEASE.
CAB LICENSE
RORY CONALL

AS LUCK WOULD HAVE IT, THAT'S *MY* HOTEL!
IT'S BEEN IN THE FAMILY FOR GENERATIONS!
YOU MUST BE THE O'CONNELL FAMILY? ROBERT, LAUREN, LILY, AND TYLER.
AND REMEMBER TO LET ALL THE COOKIES COOL TO ROOM TEMPERATURE BEFORE PACKAGING THEM.
MOM! NO WORKING!
THERE. ALL DONE.
DID YOU SEE THE ONLINE ORDER WE JUST GOT?
I'M KIDDING! I'M KIDDING! LILY, TYLER, WE GET IT. WE'RE HERE TO HAVE FUN. TOGETHER. AS A FAMILY. ***VIBING.***
DING
...
DAD!
DAD!

STARTING NOW!
BY THE WAY...WHAT ARE THE ODDS THAT WE GET INTO A TAXI DRIVEN BY THE PERSON WHO OWNS OUR HOTEL? SUPER SUS.
OH, LAD, THERE ARE NO COINCIDENCES IN IRELAND.
LILY, A *LEPRECHAUN!*
I SWEAR, HIS PANTS.
TYLER, STOP BEING SILLY. THERE'S NO SUCH THING AS LEPRECHAUNS.
OH, YOU NEVER KNOW. YOU'RE ALL IN FOR A REAL ADVENTURE IN IRELAND!
ALMOST THERE NOW.

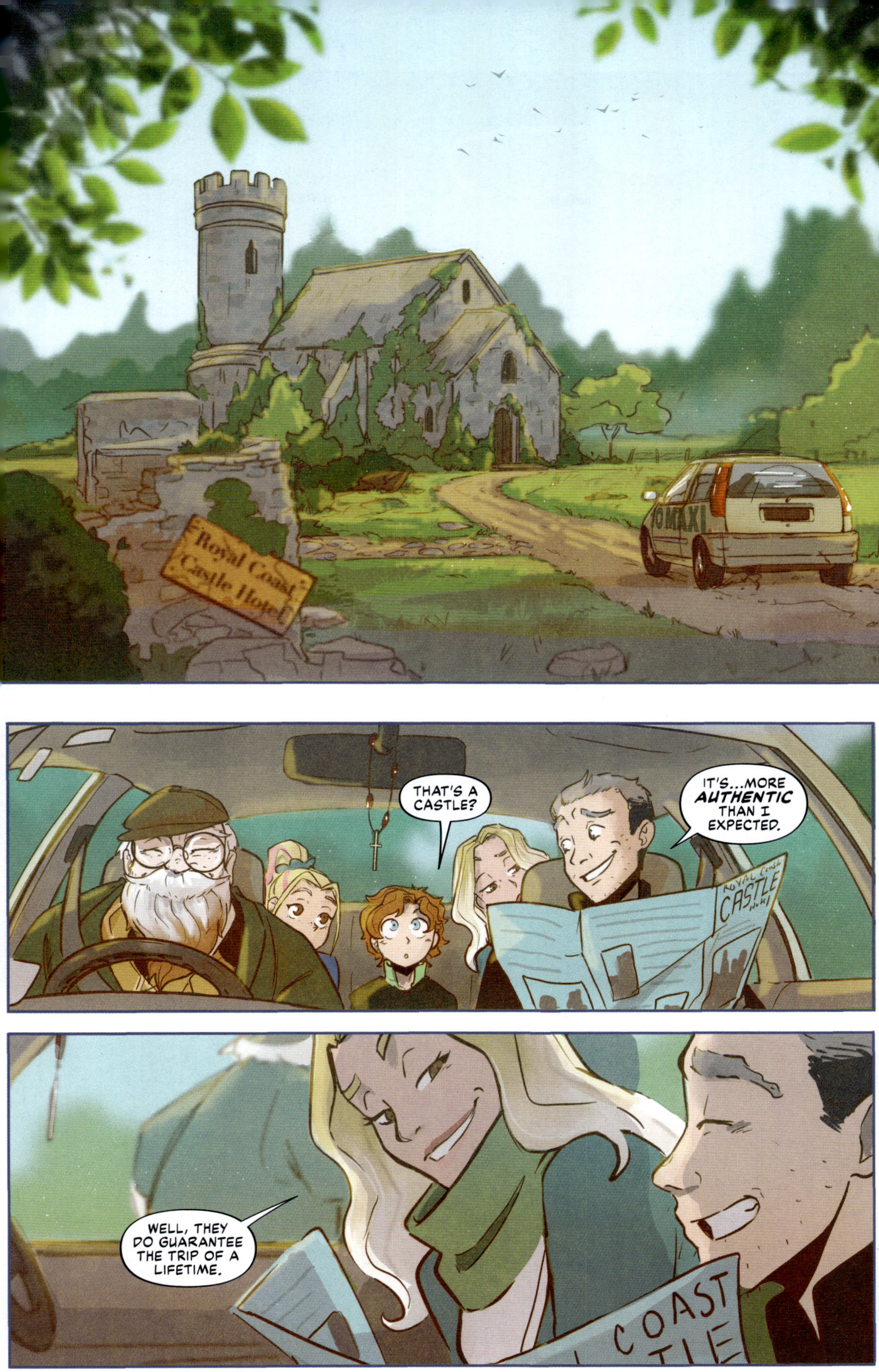
Royal Coast Castle Hotel
THAT'S A CASTLE?
IT'S...MORE **AUTHENTIC** THAN I EXPECTED.
CASTLE
WELL, THEY DO GUARANTEE THE TRIP OF A LIFETIME.
COAST

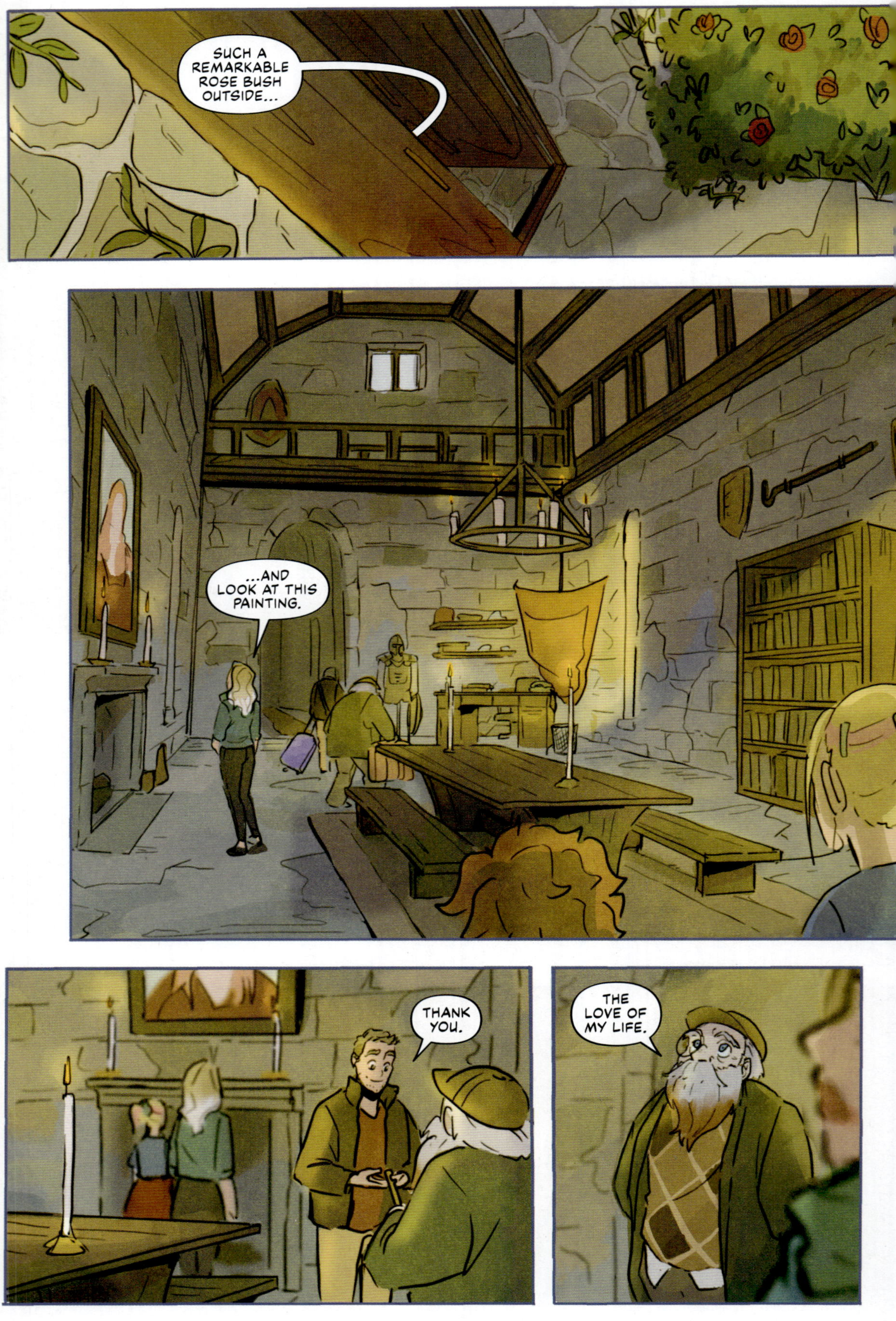
SUCH A REMARKABLE ROSE BUSH OUTSIDE...
...AND LOOK AT THIS PAINTING.
THANK YOU.
THE LOVE OF MY LIFE.

SHE'S BEAUTIFUL.
AND SHE HAS SUCH KIND EYES.
LIKE YOU.
IF I'M BEING HONEST, IT TAKES HER A WHILE TO WARM UP, WHEN YOU FIRST MEET HER.
"ONE DAY CAN CHANGE EVERY-THING."
HER FATHER USED TO TELL HER THAT. LILY, THOSE ARE WORDS TO REMEMBER.
DO YOU HAVE WIFI?

I THINK YOU'LL FIND WE'RE A BIT BEHIND THE TIMES.
IT'S BEEN QUITE A WHILE SINCE I'VE SEEN SUCH A CURIOUS BACK-PACK.
OUR LAST NAME--O'CONNELL--MEANS *DESCENDED FROM WOLVES.*
INDEED IT DOES. AND YOU LIKE PUZZLES I SEE. WELL, IF YOU'RE UP FOR A REAL CHALLENGE, I'VE GOT ONE FOR YOU.
DO YOU THINK YOU CAN PUT IT BACK TOGETHER?
CRRREAK

I'M A--
HERE WE GO.
--PUZZLE MASTER.
I DON'T KNOW, LILY. HE MAY NEED SOME HELP WITH THIS ONE.
BRRING
A LANDLINE!
OK, BOOMER. HAS THIS PLACE CHANGED IN THE LAST THOUSAND YEARS?

GOT ONE!
I HAVE A PICK UP, BUT I'LL BE BACK IN A JIFFY.
VOCAB WORD! KIDS?
IT MEANS A SHORT AMOUNT OF TIME.
NOW WHERE ARE MY...
AH, THANK YOU, LILY. AS YOU'LL FIND, EVERYTHING IS REVEALED BY TIME.
MAY THE ROAD RISE UP TO MEET YOU.
OH, RIGHT. I SHOULD SAY, BY WAY OF INTRODUCTION AND EXPLANATION...THERE'S A YOUNG MAN WHO LIVES HERE, WHO YOU'LL MEET SOON ENOUGH.
HIS NAME IS RORY, AND HE'S NOT EXACTLY EXPECTING VISITORS.

ANOTHER ONE!
WHILE THE KIDS ARE WORKING ON THAT, YOU WANT TO PEEP THE ROOM?
M'LADY.
TADA!
TYLER...I'M ***ACTUALLY*** PRETTY IMPRESSED.
LET'S TELL MOM AND DAD!

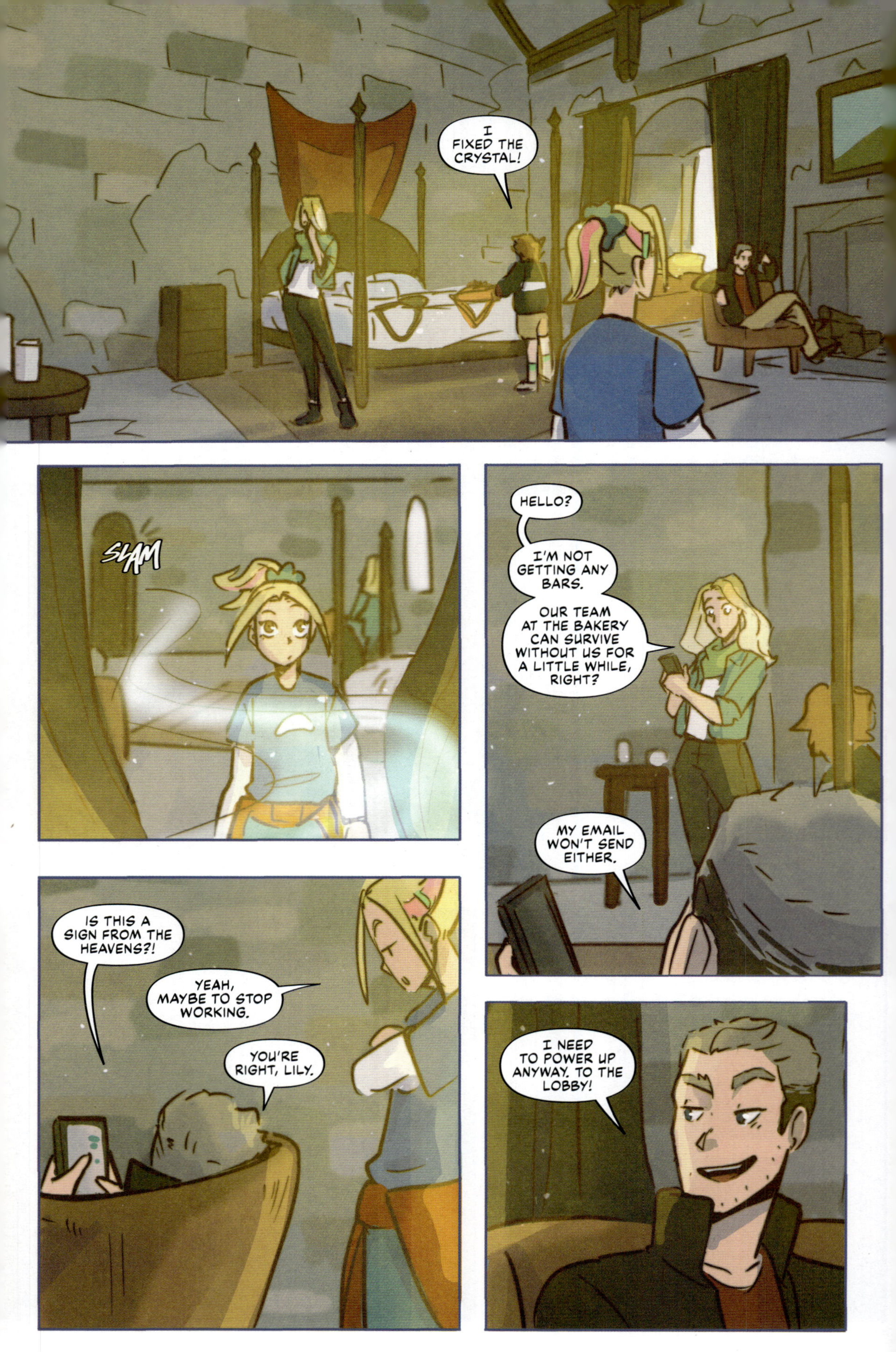
I FIXED THE CRYSTAL!
SLAM
HELLO?
I'M NOT GETTING ANY BARS.
OUR TEAM AT THE BAKERY CAN SURVIVE WITHOUT US FOR A LITTLE WHILE, RIGHT?
MY EMAIL WON'T SEND EITHER.
IS THIS A SIGN FROM THE HEAVENS?!
YEAH, MAYBE TO STOP WORKING.
YOU'RE RIGHT, LILY.
I NEED TO POWER UP ANYWAY. TO THE LOBBY!

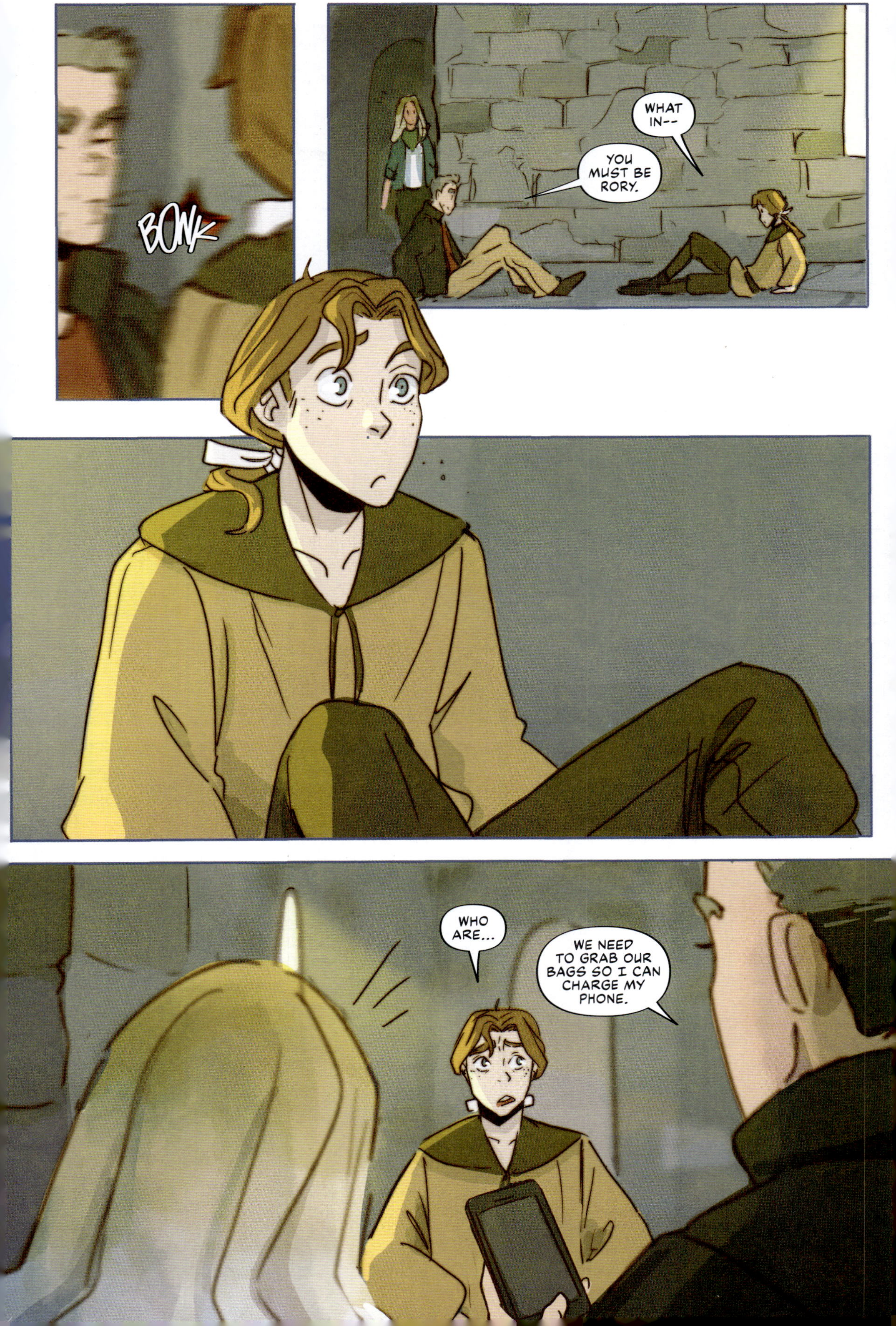
BONK
WHAT IN--
YOU MUST BE RORY.
WHO ARE...
WE NEED TO GRAB OUR BAGS SO I CAN CHARGE MY PHONE.

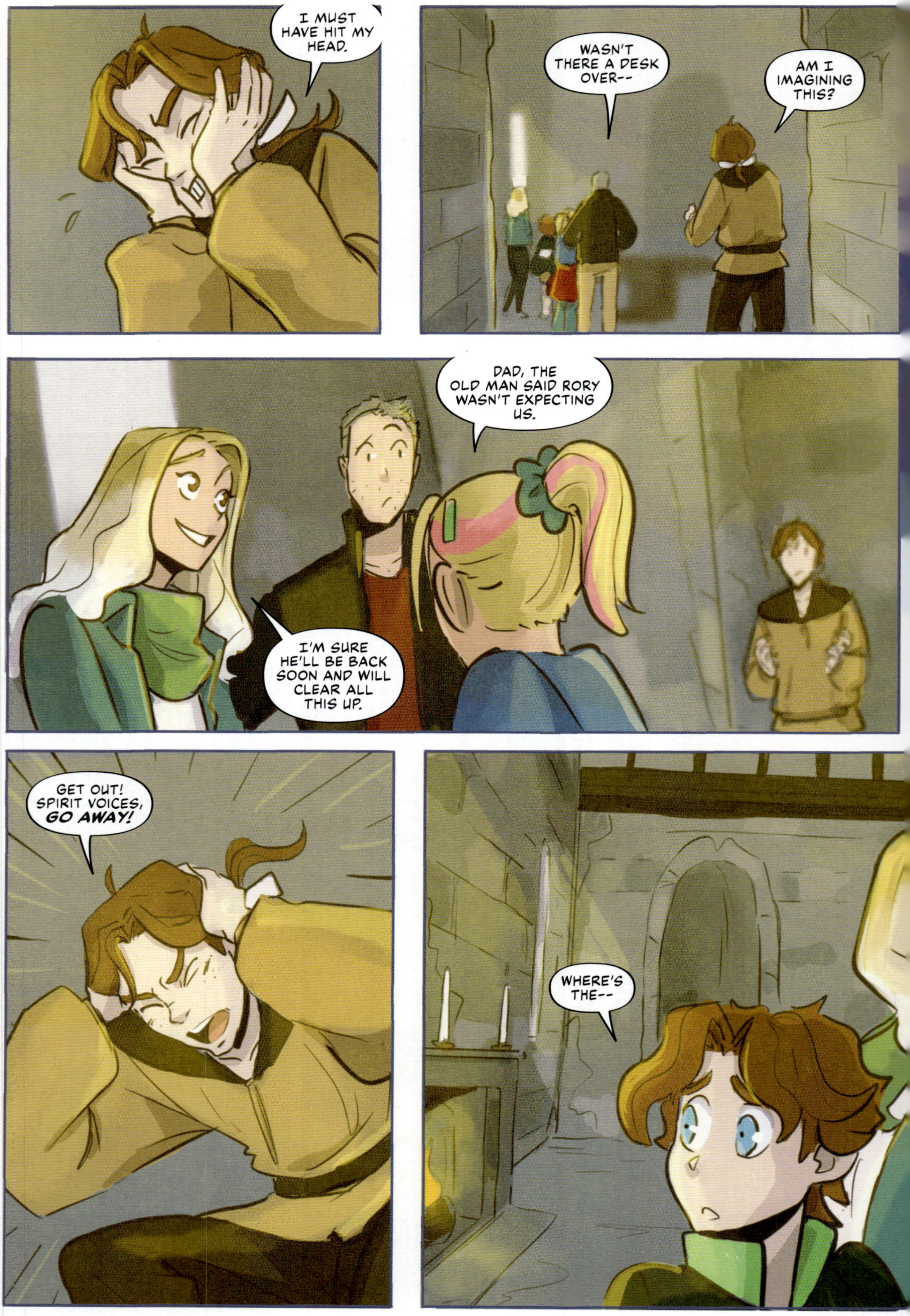
I MUST HAVE HIT MY HEAD.
WASN'T THERE A DESK OVER--
AM I IMAGINING THIS?
DAD, THE OLD MAN SAID RORY WASN'T EXPECTING US.
I'M SURE HE'LL BE BACK SOON AND WILL CLEAR ALL THIS UP.
GET OUT! SPIRIT VOICES, **GO AWAY!**
WHERE'S THE--

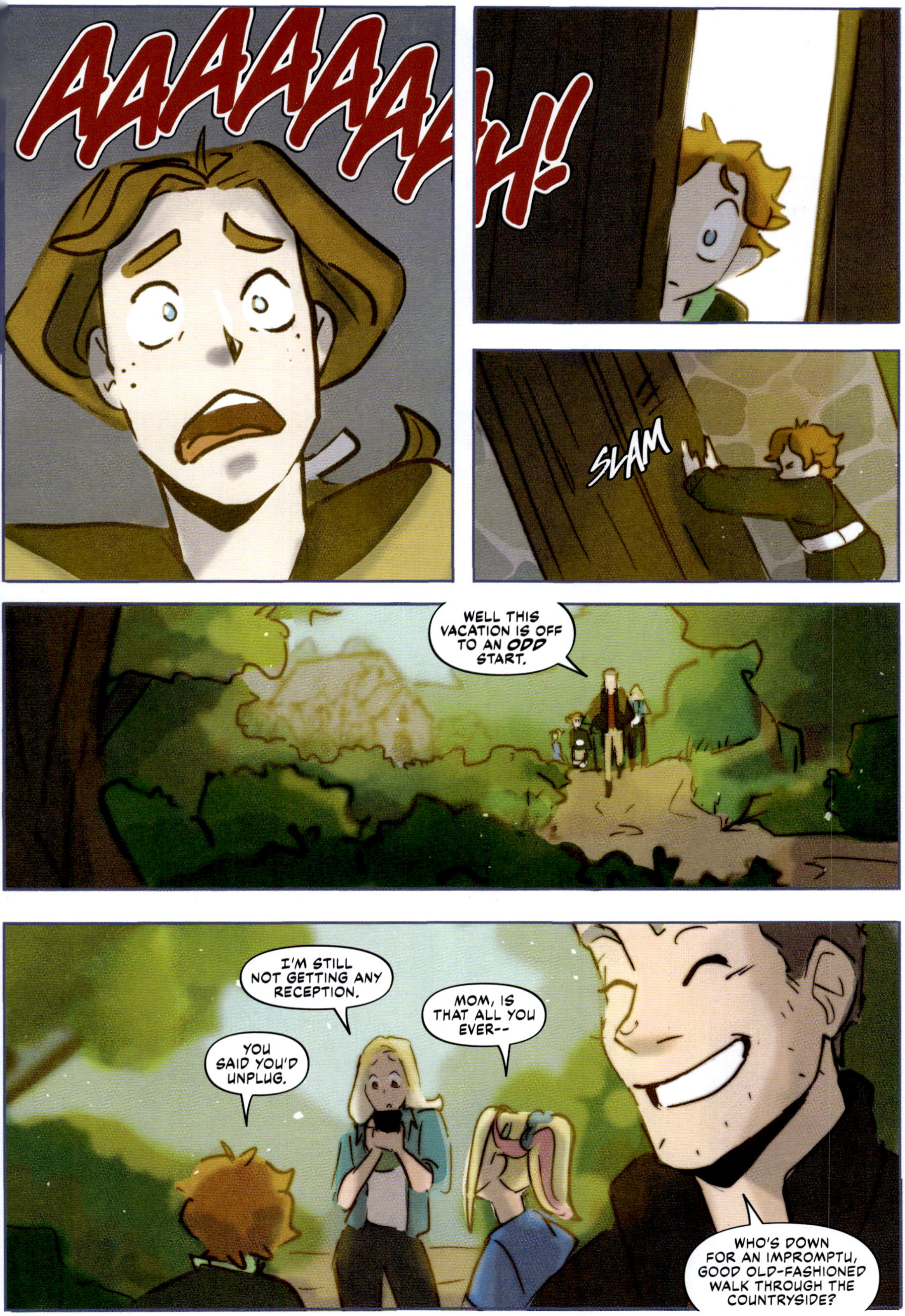
AAAAAAAH!
SLAM
WELL THIS VACATION IS OFF TO AN ODD START.
I'M STILL NOT GETTING ANY RECEPTION.
YOU SAID YOU'D UNPLUG.
MOM, IS THAT ALL YOU EVER--
WHO'S DOWN FOR AN IMPROMPTU, GOOD OLD-FASHIONED WALK THROUGH THE COUNTRYSIDE?

OK, IRELAND REALLY IS BEAUTIFUL!
DOESN'T IT FEEL LIKE WE'RE IN THE MIDDLE OF NOWHERE?
I'D PREFER A COUPLE MORE CONVENIENCE STORES...
UGH!
...BUT THIS IS NICE! WE'RE GETTING SOME QUALITY FAMILY TIME. SQUAD GOALS!
FOUR-LEAF CLOVER!
FOUND ONE?
THAT WOULD HAVE BEEN A SIGN OF GOOD LUCK.
I THOUGHT I SAW--
LYING AS ALWAYS.

ONE IN TEN THOUSAND CHANCE, BUDDY. BUT KEEP LOOKING! WE'VE GOT THE LUCK OF THE IRISH ON OUR SIDE. ESPECIALLY HERE, SINCE OUR ANCESTORS ARE FROM THIS EXACT AREA.
CAN YOU IMAGINE LIVING HERE BACK THEN?
NO EMAILS!
NO STRESS RUNNING A FAMILY COOKIE COMPANY.
NO INDOOR PLUMBING?
POTATOES FOR EVERY MEAL.
ACTUALLY, NO. POTATOES WERE ONLY INTRODUCED IN IRELAND IN THE LATE 1500s. READ THAT ON THE PLANE ON THE WAY HERE! BEFORE THAT, PEOPLE FARMED CARROTS AND CABBAGE AND WHEAT.
WHEAT MAKES FLOUR.
AND FLOUR MAKES COOKIES!
ALL THIS TALK OF FOOD IS MAKING ME HUNGRY! WHO'S UP FOR SOME LUNCH?

HI THERE.
GOOD AFTERNOON.
CAN YOU POINT US TO THE NEAREST PUB?
T.Y.S.M.

ON THE PLANE, I READ AN ARTICLE ABOUT NEW ***HISTORICAL RE-ENACTMENTS.*** YEAH, IT'S A HOT, NEW TREND IN TOURISM.
LIKE THE JAMESTOWN SETTLEMENT IN VIRGINIA?
OR THE PLYMOUTH COLONY ONE IN MASSACHUSETTS?
EXACTLY! THEY APPARENTLY HAVE THEM ALL OVER THE PLACE NOW.
LOOKS LIKE WE'VE STUMBLED INTO ONE. THAT EXPLAINS THE WAGON AND THE CLOTHES.
CRRRK

CAN I GRAB A COUPLE OF MENUS PLEASE?
YOU NEED TO PLAY ALONG.
OH, RIGHT!
MY GOOD SIR. TWO OF YOUR FINEST MEADS. AND TWO WATERS FOR THE KIDS.
BOTTLES, IF YOU ALLOW THEM HERE.

SLÁINTE, AS THEY SAY HERE.
AUTHENTIC.
IT REALLY IS QUITE AMAZING.
THERE WERE A LOT MORE TOURISTS WHEN MY CLASS VISITED COLONIAL WILLIAMSBURG.
I DON'T THINK I READ ABOUT THIS ONE IN ANY OF THE TOUR GUIDES. MUST BE NEW.
BET YOU DIDN'T THINK YOUR OL' PARENTS WERE AHEAD OF THE TIMES. STRAIGHT FACTS, BAE AND I ARE BUSSIN'.
PLEASE STOP DOING THAT.
SKREECH

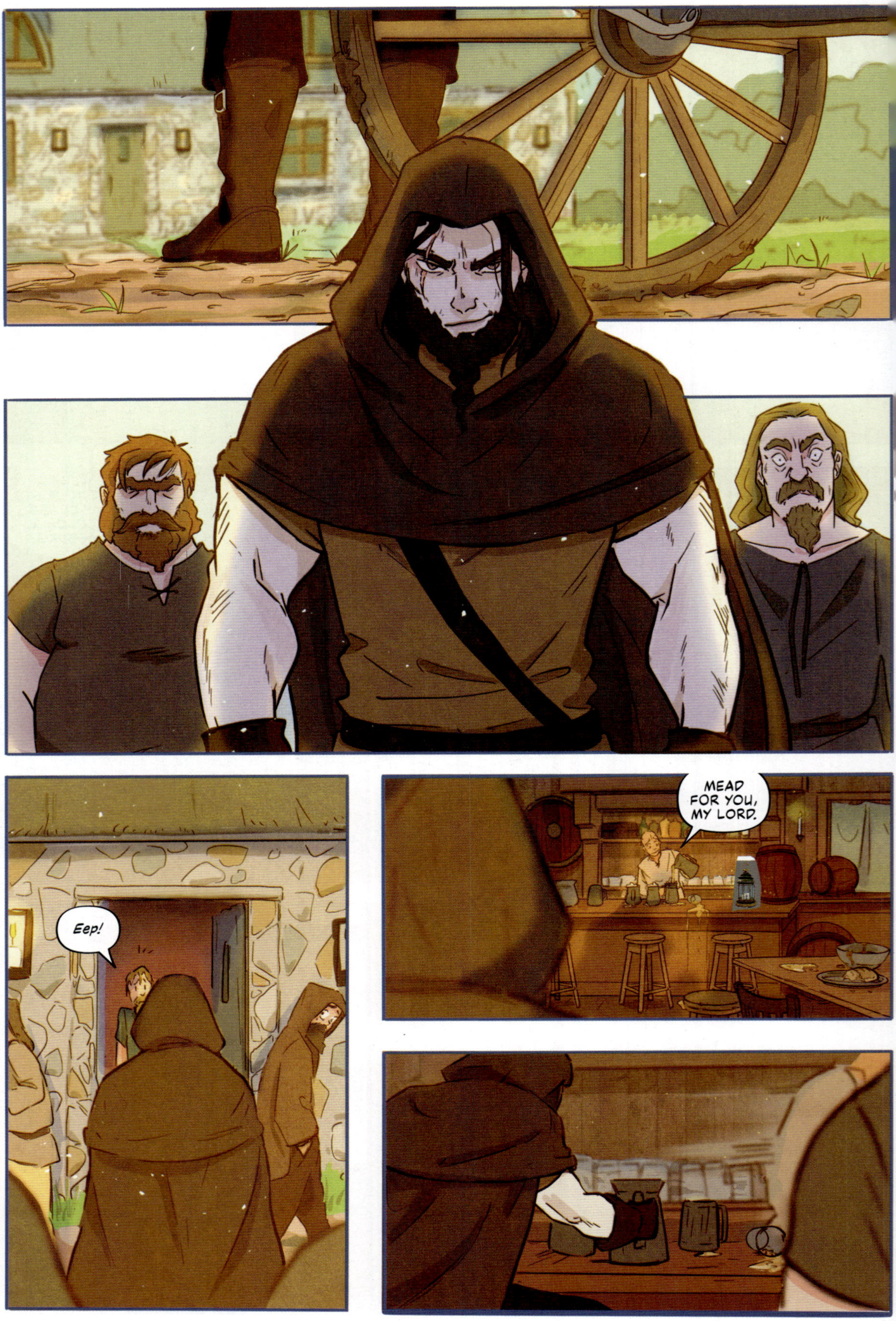
Eep!
MEAD FOR YOU, MY LORD.

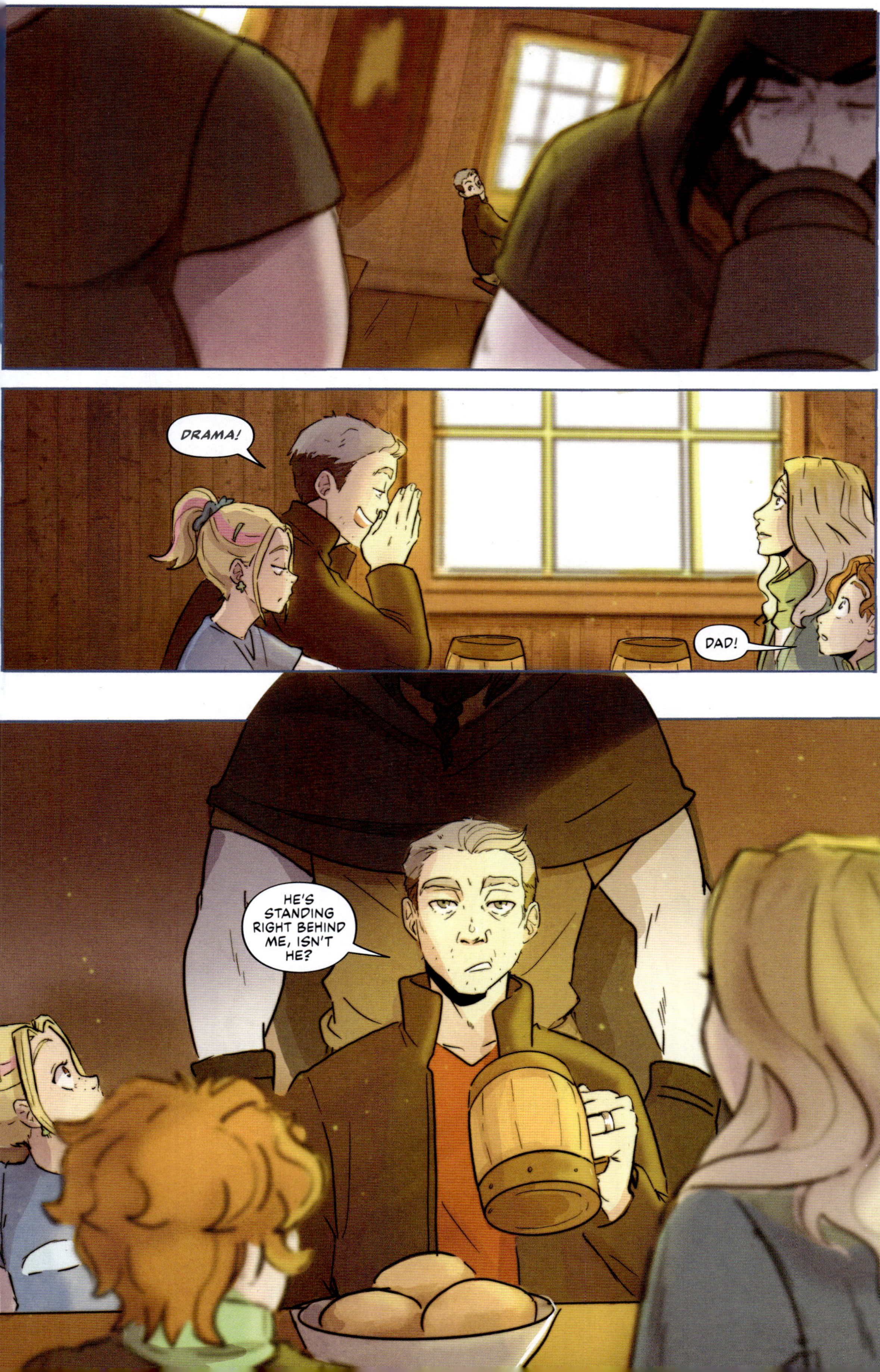
DRAMA!
DAD!
HE'S STANDING RIGHT BEHIND ME, ISN'T HE?

#2 MAIN COVER BY **ASIAH FULMORE**

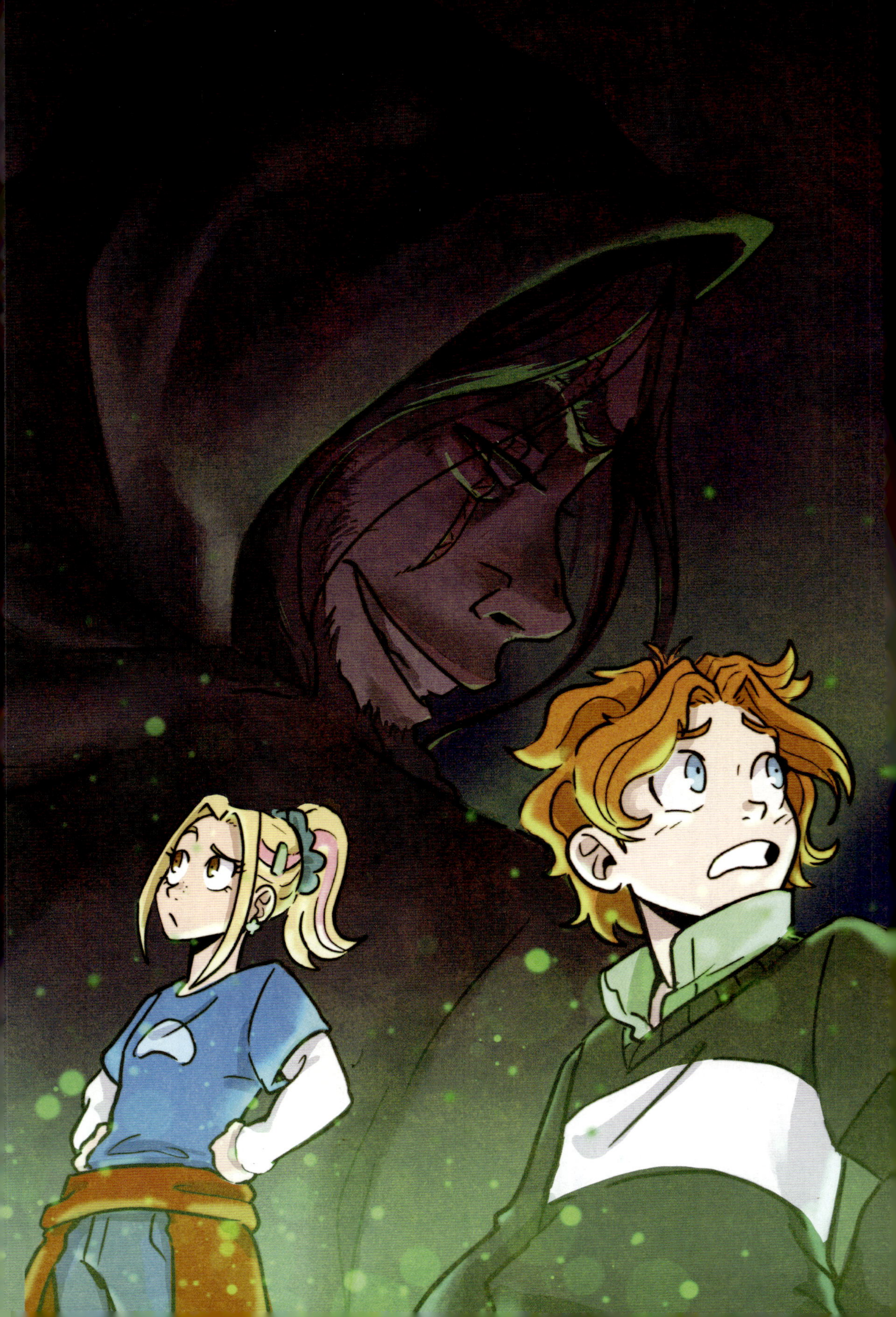

YEP... HE'S STANDING RIGHT BEHIND ME.
GRRR...
GIVE ME SOME DAP!
GUESS FIST-BUMPING HASN'T BEEN INVENTED YET, KIDS?
I WAS TOLD THERE WERE... **FAIR FOLK** VISITING.
WELL, THESE KIDS ARE OFTEN **CLOWNING!**

YOU APPEAR TO HAVE JOURNEYED... FAR.
WE'RE FROM THE STATES.
WHICH THE VIKINGS MAY NOT HAVE DISCOVERED YET.
YOU'RE *VIKINGS?*
NO, NO.
WE'RE FROM...
...A LAND BEYOND THE SEA.

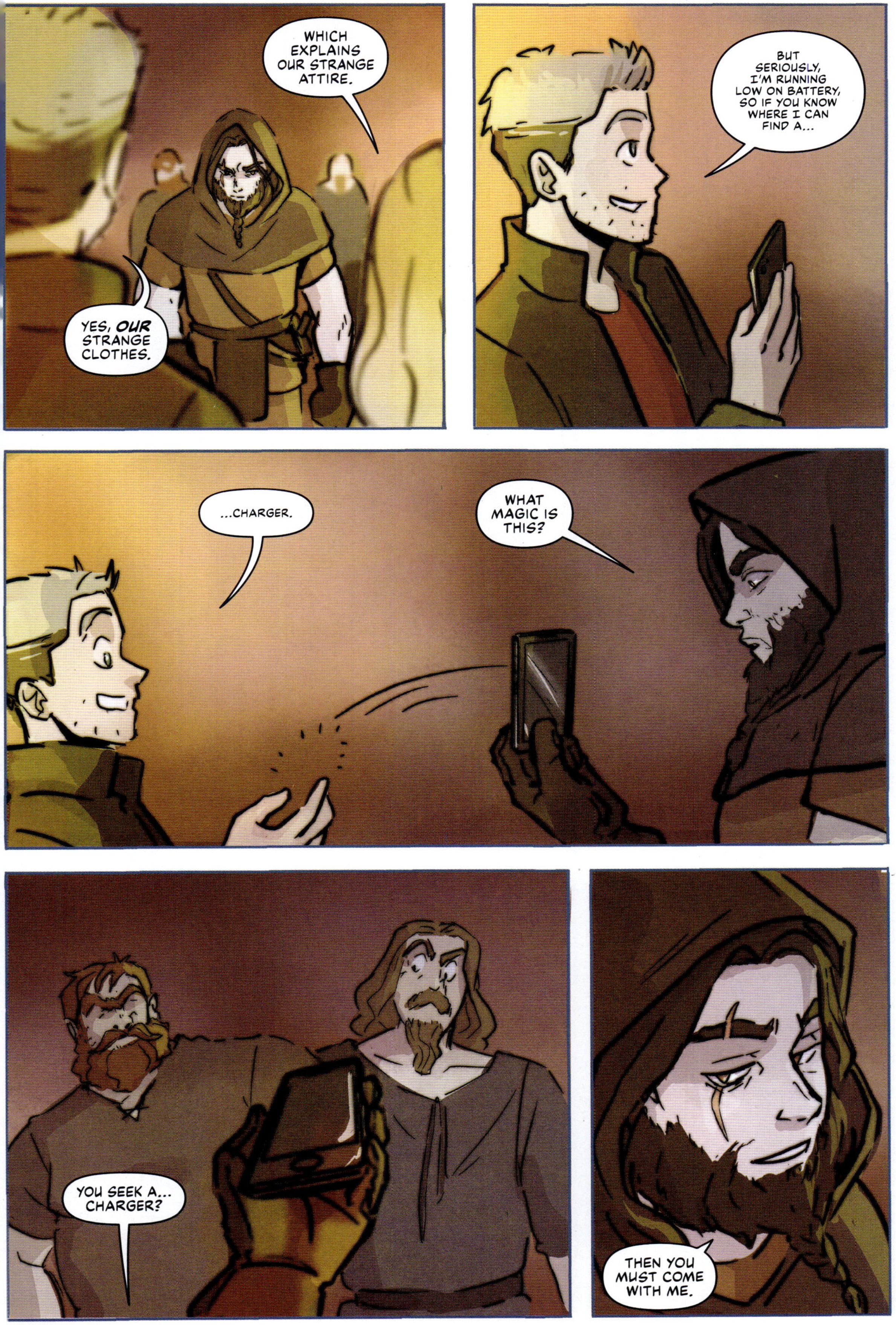
WHICH EXPLAINS OUR STRANGE ATTIRE.
YES, OUR STRANGE CLOTHES.
BUT SERIOUSLY, I'M RUNNING LOW ON BATTERY, SO IF YOU KNOW WHERE I CAN FIND A...
...CHARGER.
WHAT MAGIC IS THIS?
YOU SEEK A... CHARGER?
THEN YOU MUST COME WITH ME.

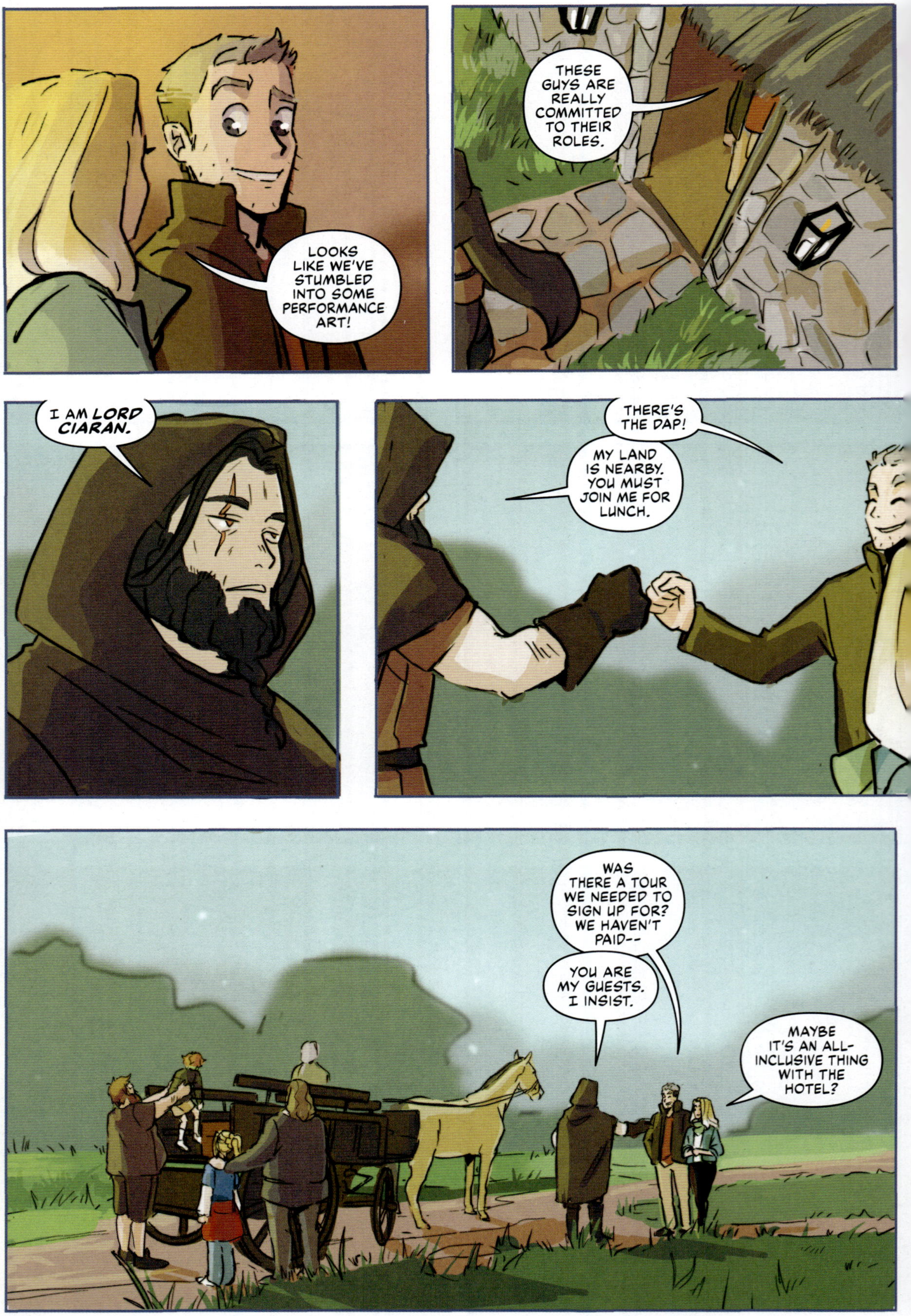
LOOKS LIKE WE'VE STUMBLED INTO SOME PERFORMANCE ART!
THESE GUYS ARE REALLY COMMITTED TO THEIR ROLES.
I AM **LORD CIARAN.**
MY LAND IS NEARBY. YOU MUST JOIN ME FOR LUNCH.
THERE'S THE DAP!
WAS THERE A TOUR WE NEEDED TO SIGN UP FOR? WE HAVEN'T PAID--
YOU ARE MY GUESTS. I INSIST.
MAYBE IT'S AN ALL-INCLUSIVE THING WITH THE HOTEL?

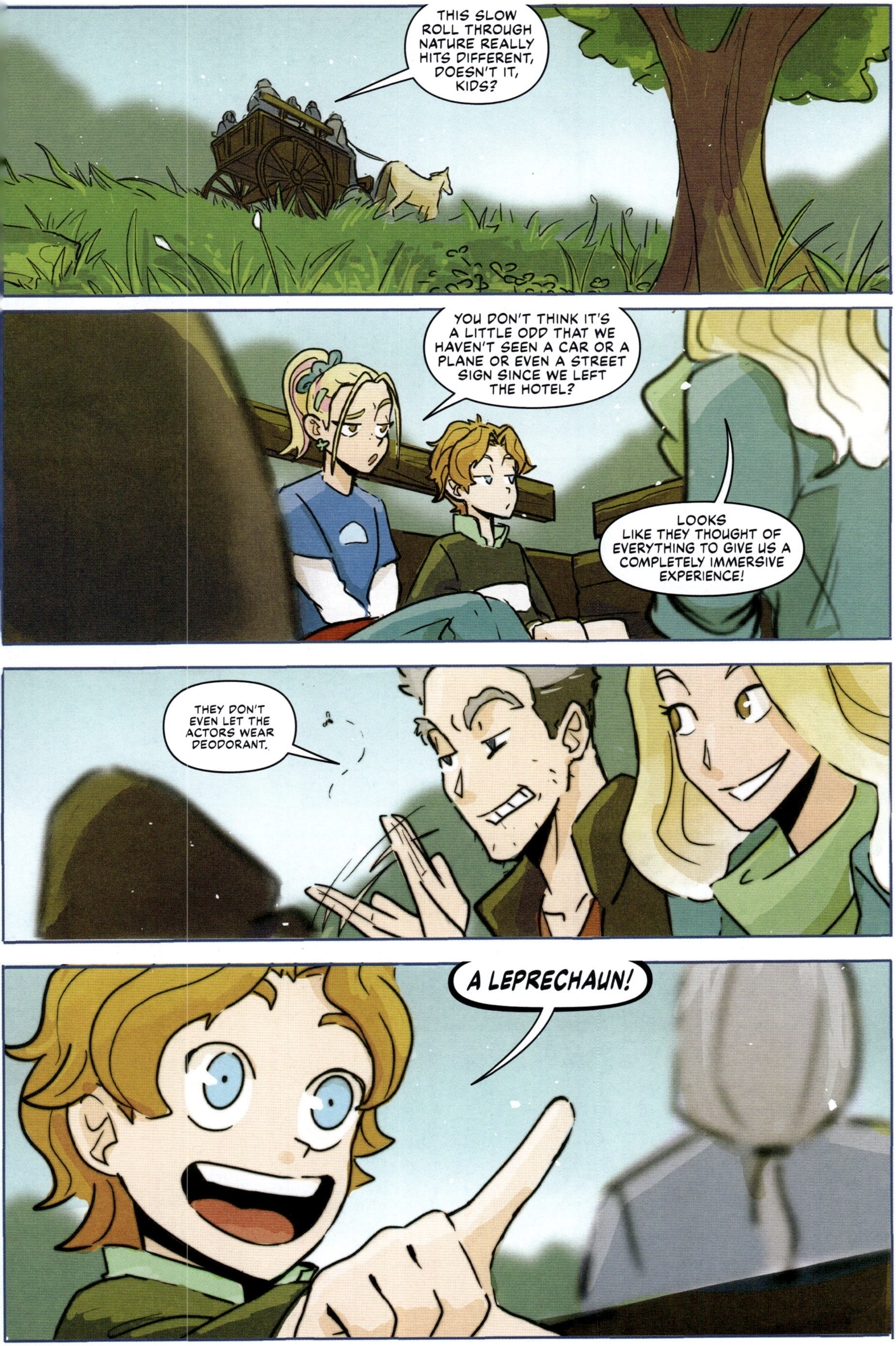
THIS SLOW ROLL THROUGH NATURE REALLY HITS DIFFERENT, DOESN'T IT, KIDS?
YOU DON'T THINK IT'S A LITTLE ODD THAT WE HAVEN'T SEEN A CAR OR A PLANE OR EVEN A STREET SIGN SINCE WE LEFT THE HOTEL?
LOOKS LIKE THEY THOUGHT OF EVERYTHING TO GIVE US A COMPLETELY IMMERSIVE EXPERIENCE!
THEY DON'T EVEN LET THE ACTORS WEAR DEODORANT.
A LEPRECHAUN!

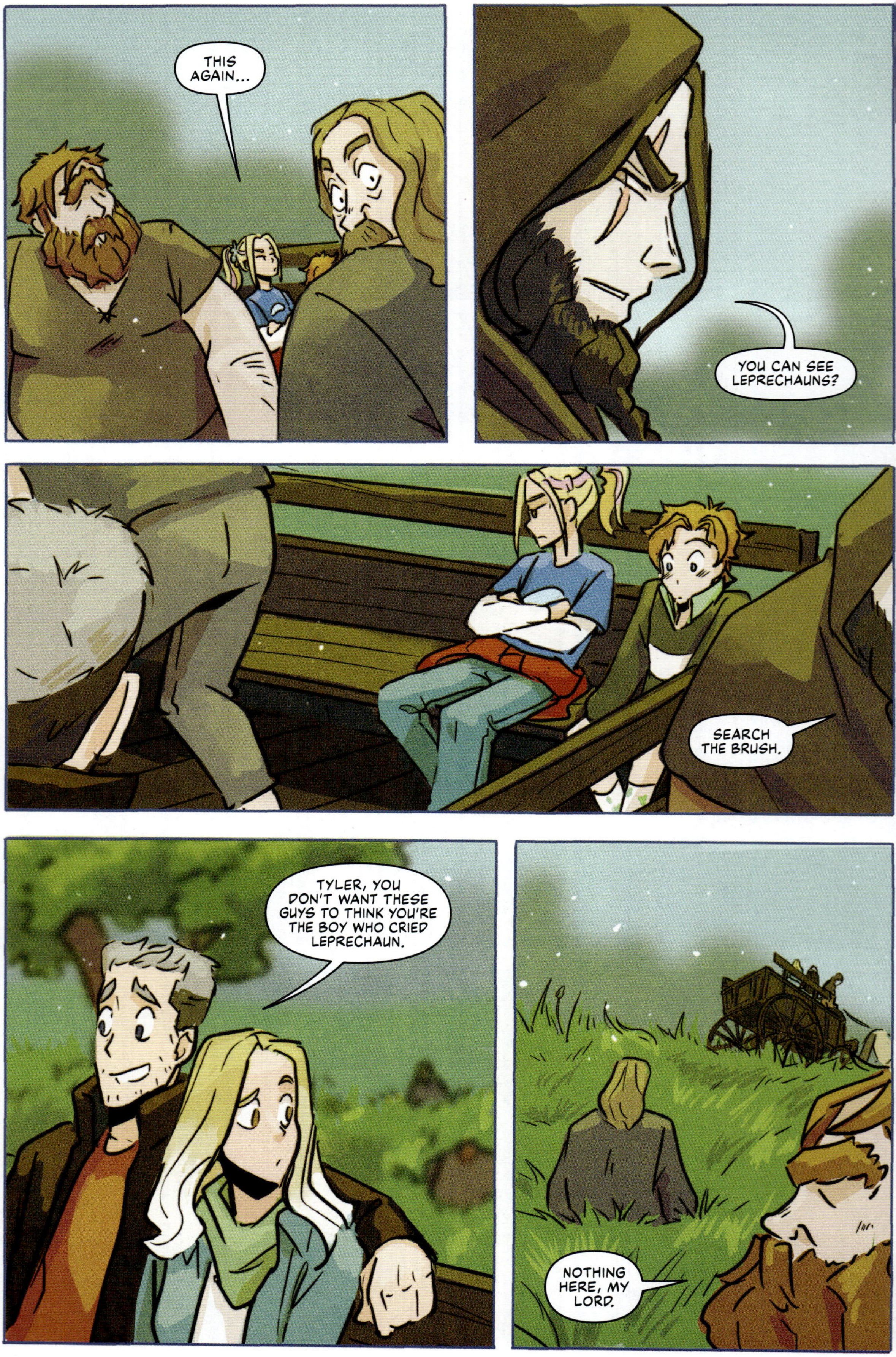

THIS AGAIN...
YOU CAN SEE LEPRECHAUNS?
SEARCH THE BRUSH.
TYLER, YOU DON'T WANT THESE GUYS TO THINK YOU'RE THE BOY WHO CRIED LEPRECHAUN.
NOTHING HERE, MY LORD.

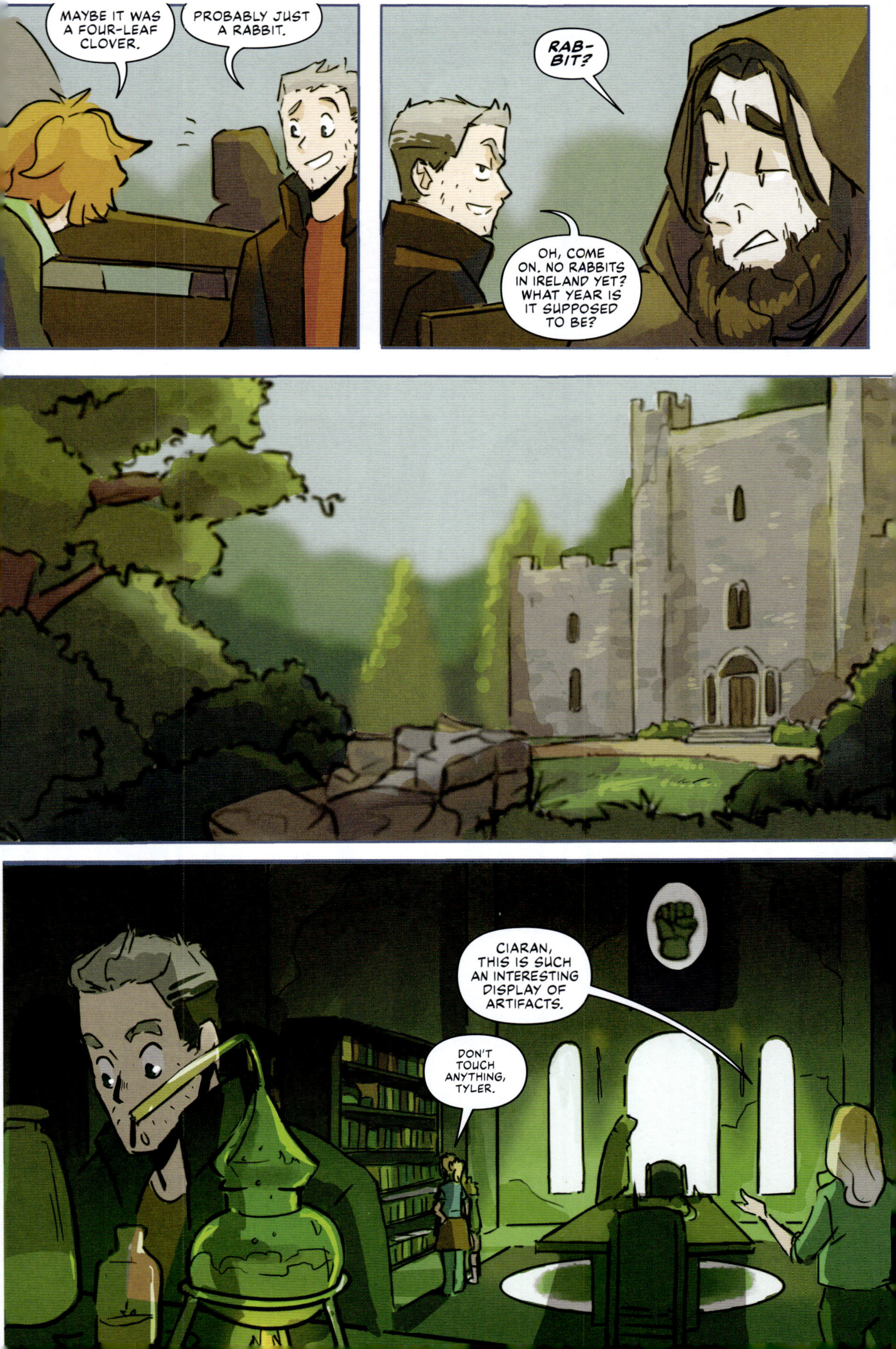
MAYBE IT WAS A FOUR-LEAF CLOVER.
PROBABLY JUST A RABBIT.
RAB-BIT?
OH, COME ON. NO RABBITS IN IRELAND YET? WHAT YEAR IS IT SUPPOSED TO BE?
CIARAN, THIS IS SUCH AN INTERESTING DISPLAY OF ARTIFACTS.
DON'T TOUCH ANYTHING, TYLER.

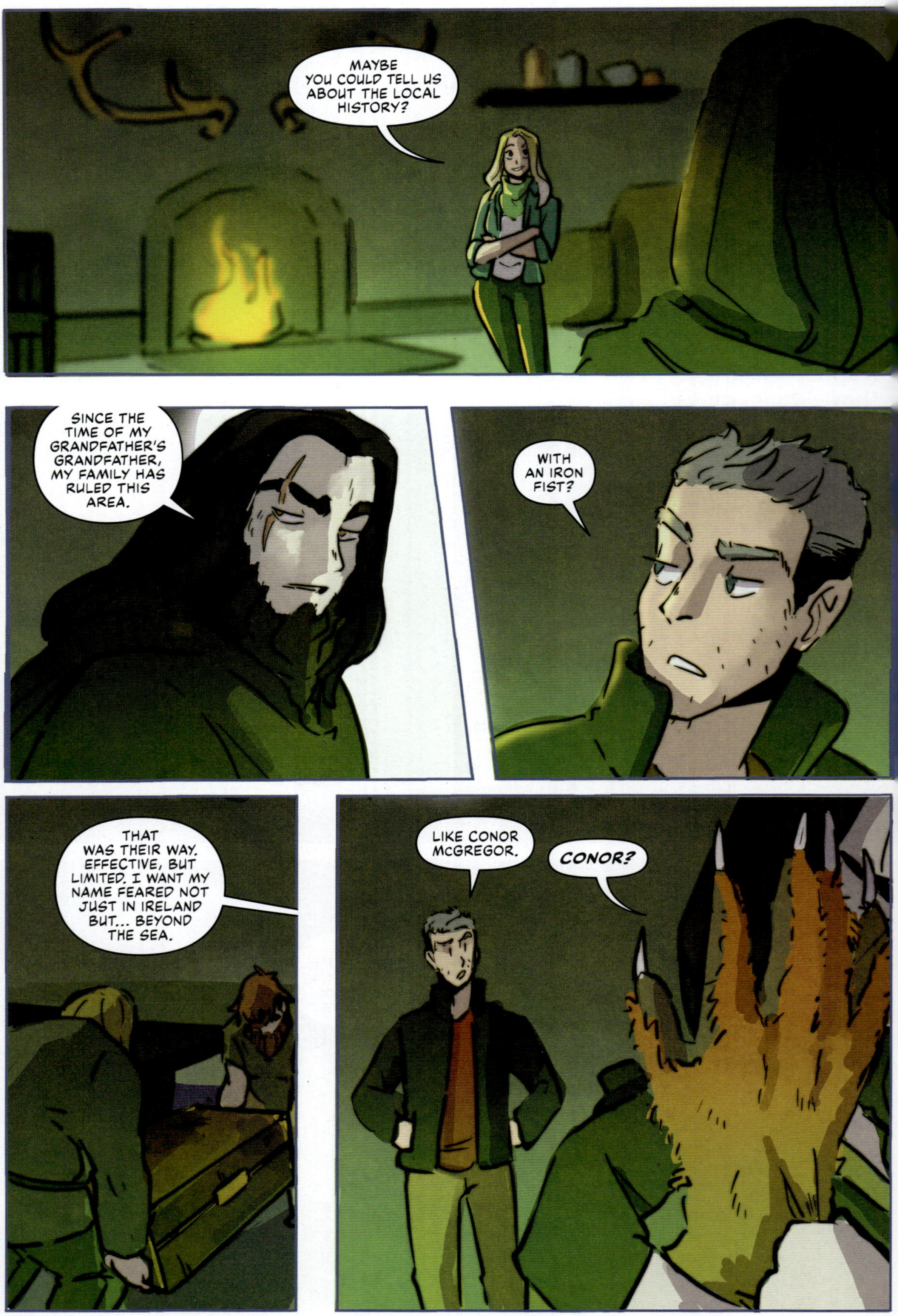
MAYBE YOU COULD TELL US ABOUT THE LOCAL HISTORY?
SINCE THE TIME OF MY GRANDFATHER'S GRANDFATHER, MY FAMILY HAS RULED THIS AREA.
WITH AN IRON FIST?
THAT WAS THEIR WAY. EFFECTIVE, BUT LIMITED. I WANT MY NAME FEARED NOT JUST IN IRELAND BUT... BEYOND THE SEA.
LIKE CONOR MCGREGOR.
CONOR?

I FEAR NO *WOLVES.*
LILY, OUR LAST NAME MEANS--
IN HIS PRIME?
MAN, HE COULD FIGHT.
ONE DAY, YOUR MOUTH WILL BREAK YOUR NOSE.
NOT A FAN, I GUESS.

YOU ARE HERE ON A TRULY AUSPICIOUS DAY.
VOCAB WORD!
"PROMISING SUCCESS."
I AM A MAN OF EDUCATION. I HAVE MASTERED POTIONS AND ELIXIRS.
I HAVE READ OF THE EMPERORS OF ROME AND THE KINGS AND QUEENS OF EGYPT.
AND MAYBE JUST A LITTLE ***GAME OF THRONES,*** TOO.
YOU THINK THIS IS A GAME?
I HAVE SPENT MY LIFE SEARCHING FOR THAT.

HE'S DR. McSCRUFFLEFINGERS!
AND JUST WHEN I FINALLY HAVE IT...
...THE BLOOD FROM THE CONQUEST STILL FRESH...
...HERE YOU ARE, TOO. ON THE SAME DAY, AT THE SAME HOUR, ON THE VERY SAME WAGON.
GROSS!
IT'S KETCHUP.
MAYBE IT'S FATE?
IN ALL MY TRAVELS, I NEVER MET YOUR KIND.
AND I NEVER HEARD OF ANYTHING LIKE THIS.

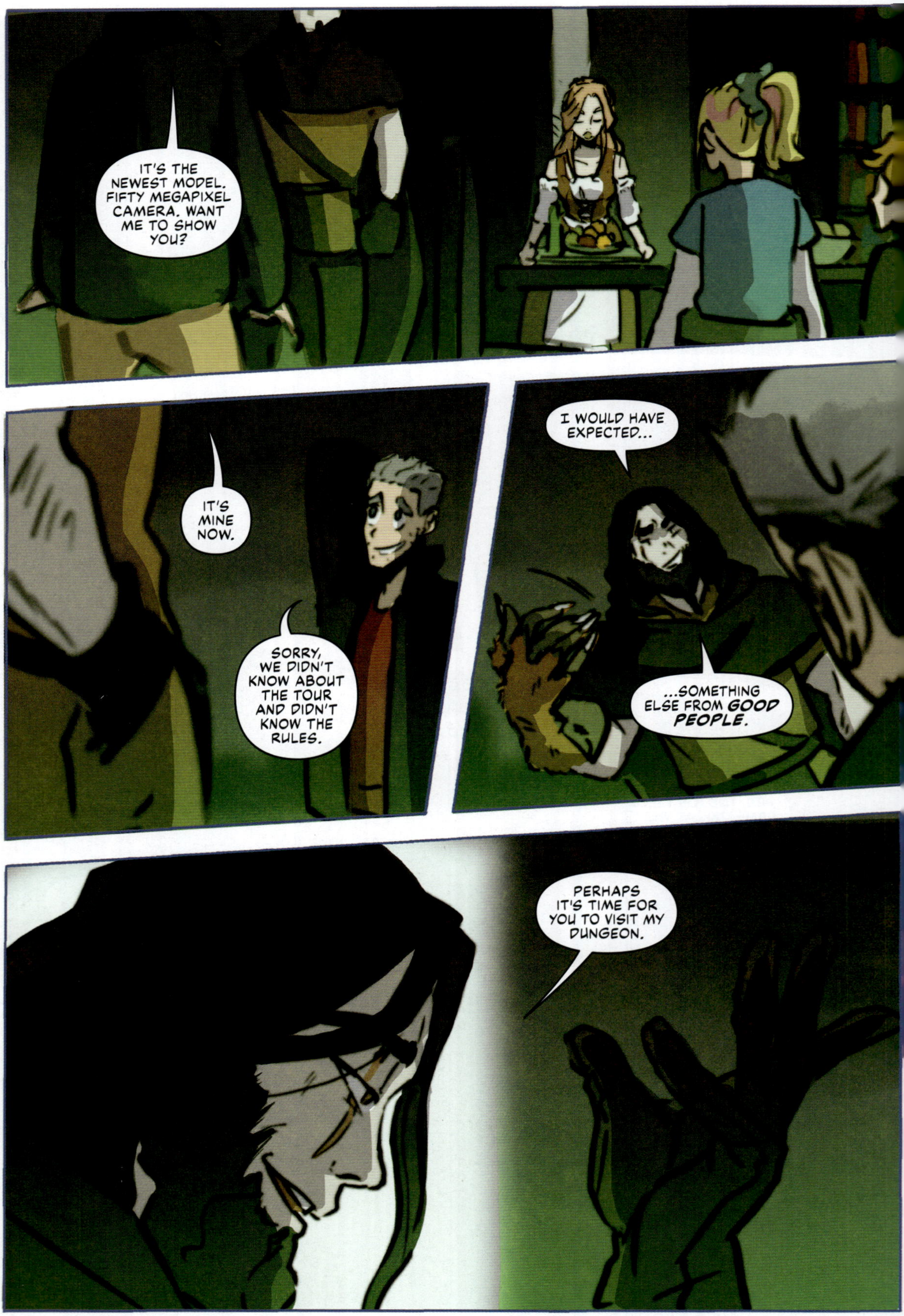
IT'S THE NEWEST MODEL. FIFTY MEGAPIXEL CAMERA. WANT ME TO SHOW YOU?
IT'S MINE NOW.
SORRY, WE DIDN'T KNOW ABOUT THE TOUR AND DIDN'T KNOW THE RULES.
I WOULD HAVE EXPECTED...
...SOMETHING ELSE FROM GOOD PEOPLE.
PERHAPS IT'S TIME FOR YOU TO VISIT MY DUNGEON.

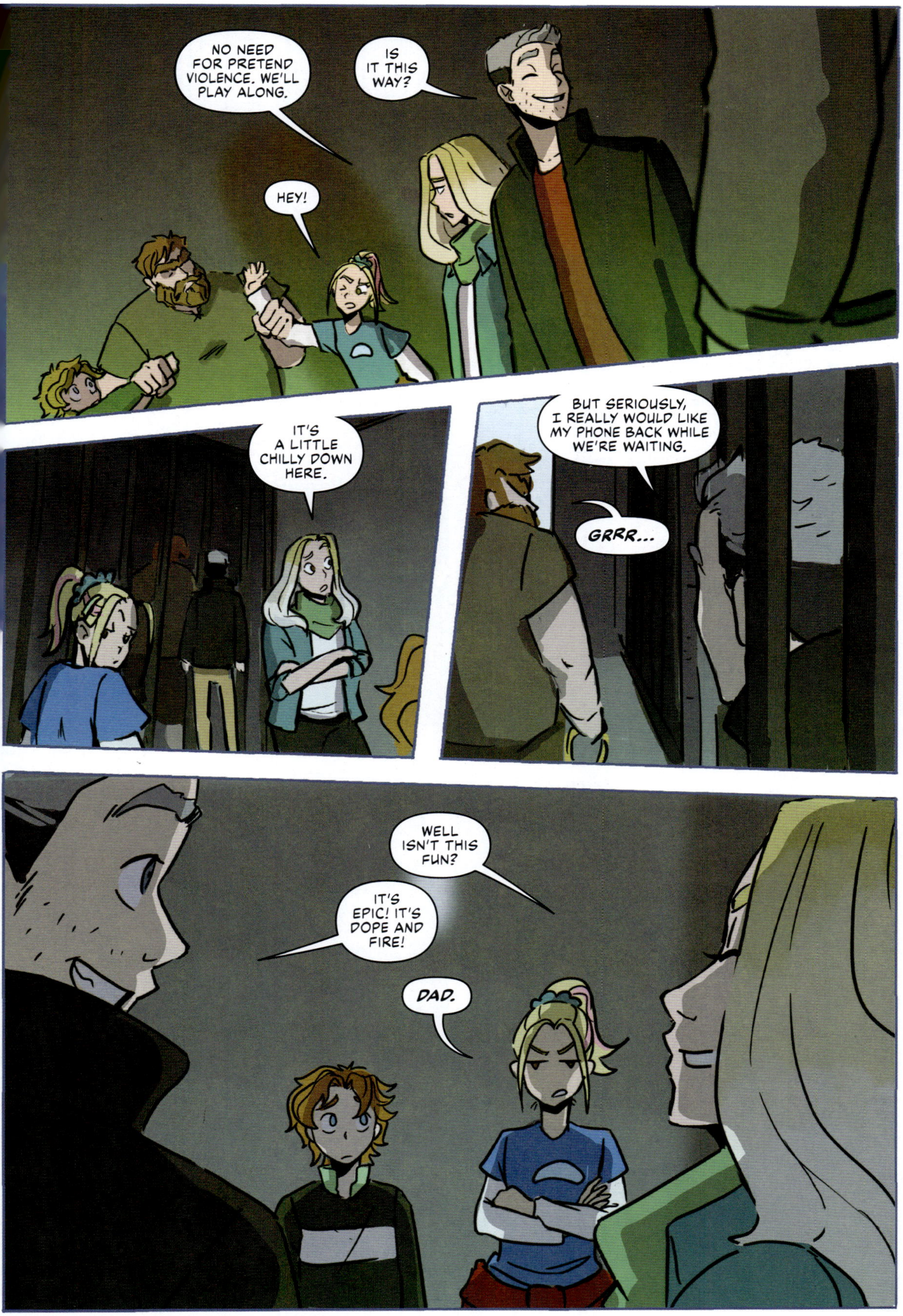
NO NEED FOR PRETEND VIOLENCE. WE'LL PLAY ALONG.
IS IT THIS WAY?
HEY!
IT'S A LITTLE CHILLY DOWN HERE.
BUT SERIOUSLY, I REALLY WOULD LIKE MY PHONE BACK WHILE WE'RE WAITING.
GRRR...
WELL ISN'T THIS FUN?
IT'S EPIC! IT'S DOPE AND FIRE!
DAD.

DID THE GIRL THAT BROUGHT THE FOOD LOOK LIKE THE WOMAN IN THE PORTRAIT AT OUR HOTEL?
ARE YOU FEELING OKAY?
I'LL BET SHE'S JET-LAGGED.
SHE'S PROBABLY HUNGRY. WE NEVER DID GET ANY LUNCH.
ACTUALLY, I THINK LILY MIGHT BE ON TO SOMETHING.
AND NOW TYLER TOO. LAUREN, DO YOU HAVE ANY SNACKS ON YOU?
I LEFT MY PURSE IN THE ROOM. WE NEED TO TELL THAT NICE OLD MAN TO GIVE PEOPLE A HEADS UP NEXT TIME.
SOME OF THE THINGS LILY SAID EARLIER--
THAT'S GOING IN THE TRIP ADVISOR REVIEW.
LET TYLER FINISH.
DEFENDING YOUR BROTHER FOR A CHANGE. NICE!

THIS PLACE DOESN'T HAVE LIGHTS.
WE HAVEN'T SEEN ANY CARS.
WHAT IF... THIS IS ALL REAL.
LIKE, WHAT IF THIS ISN'T A REENACTMENT?
EXACTLY.
OH, OKAY, PUZZLE MASTER.
I WAS JUST GOING TO SAY I THINK THE LADY FROM THE PAINTING--WHO REALLY WAS UPSTAIRS TOO--PROBABLY PLAYS A BIGGER ROLE IN THIS THAN WE THINK.
I'M SURE OF IT.
FAMILY, BRACE YOURSELVES.
WE TRAVELLED BACK IN TIME!
HAHAHAHAHAHAHAHA!
DEFINITELY NOT.
THIS IS ALL FOR FUN.

DID YOU SEE HOW CIARAN REACTED WHEN HE SAW YOUR IPHONE?
IT'S AN ANACHRONISM.
TYLER, DAD BROKE THE RULES.
GOOD VOCABULARY WORD! DO YOU KNOW IT?
I'M NOT 11.
HEY!
THEY DIDN'T HAVE CELL PHONES... **WHENEVER** WE'RE SUPPOSED TO BE.
I DIDN'T MAJOR IN HISTORY.
AROUND THE YEAR 1000?
I'M **NOT** LYING!
AW, BUDDY.
LOOK, WE'VE TALKED ABOUT THIS BEFORE. YOU DO HAVE A TENDENCY TO STRETCH THE TRUTH FROM TIME TO TIME...
ON THIS ONE, WE DON'T THINK YOU'RE **TRYING** TO LIE...
YOU'RE JUST... WRONG.

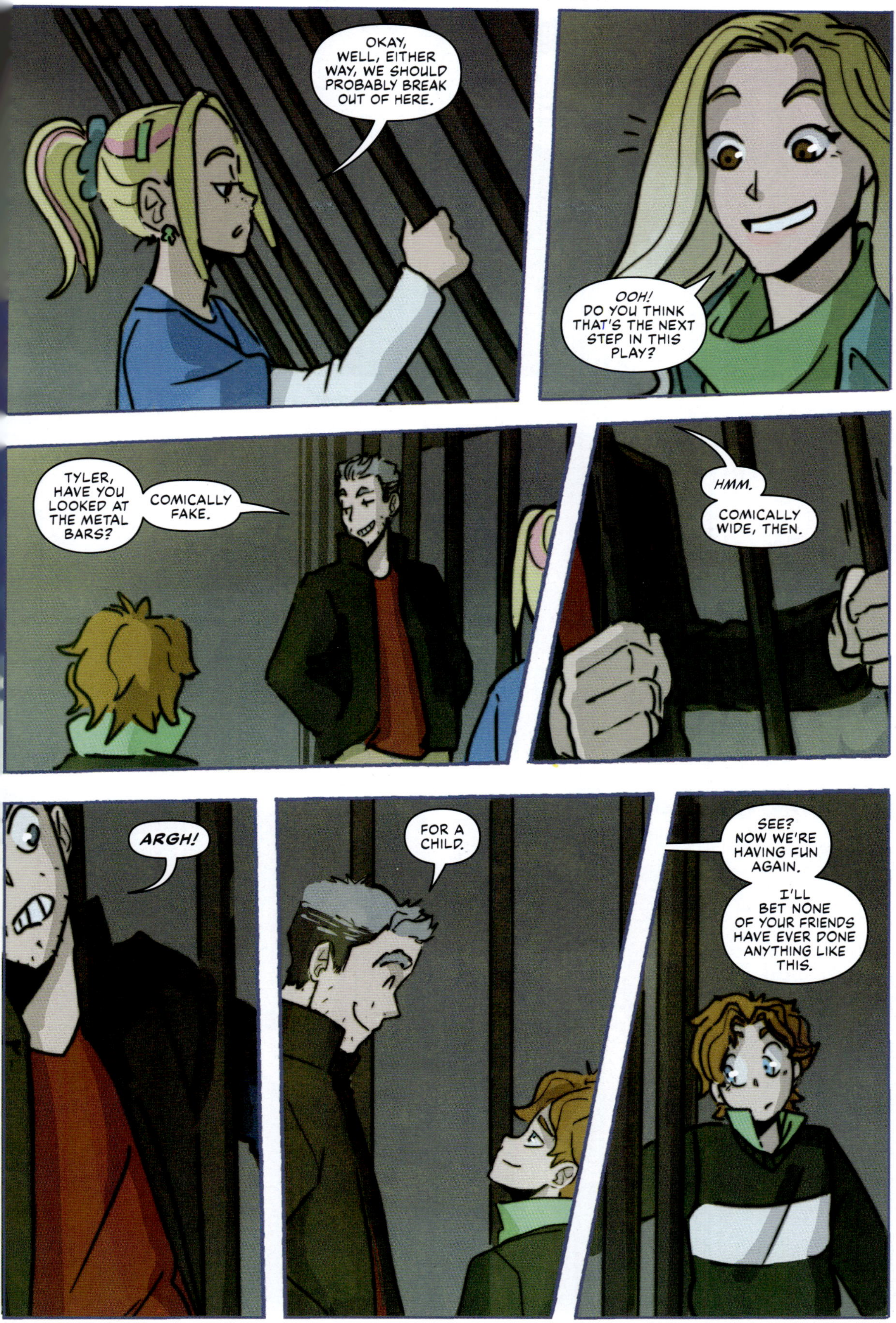
OKAY, WELL, EITHER WAY, WE SHOULD PROBABLY BREAK OUT OF HERE.
OOH! DO YOU THINK THAT'S THE NEXT STEP IN THIS PLAY?
TYLER, HAVE YOU LOOKED AT THE METAL BARS?
COMICALLY FAKE.
HMM.
COMICALLY WIDE, THEN.
ARGH!
FOR A CHILD.
SEE? NOW WE'RE HAVING FUN AGAIN.
I'LL BET NONE OF YOUR FRIENDS HAVE EVER DONE ANYTHING LIKE THIS.

SO I'M SURE YOU JUST SNEAK UPSTAIRS AND GRAB THE KEYS TO FREE US.
THEN MAYBE WE EAT THAT LUNCH THE LADY BROUGHT OUT? NOT SURE I WANT ANY MORE OF THAT MEAD.
WELL... GO ON, KIDDOS! SAVE US!
THEY'RE PROBABLY IN THERE.

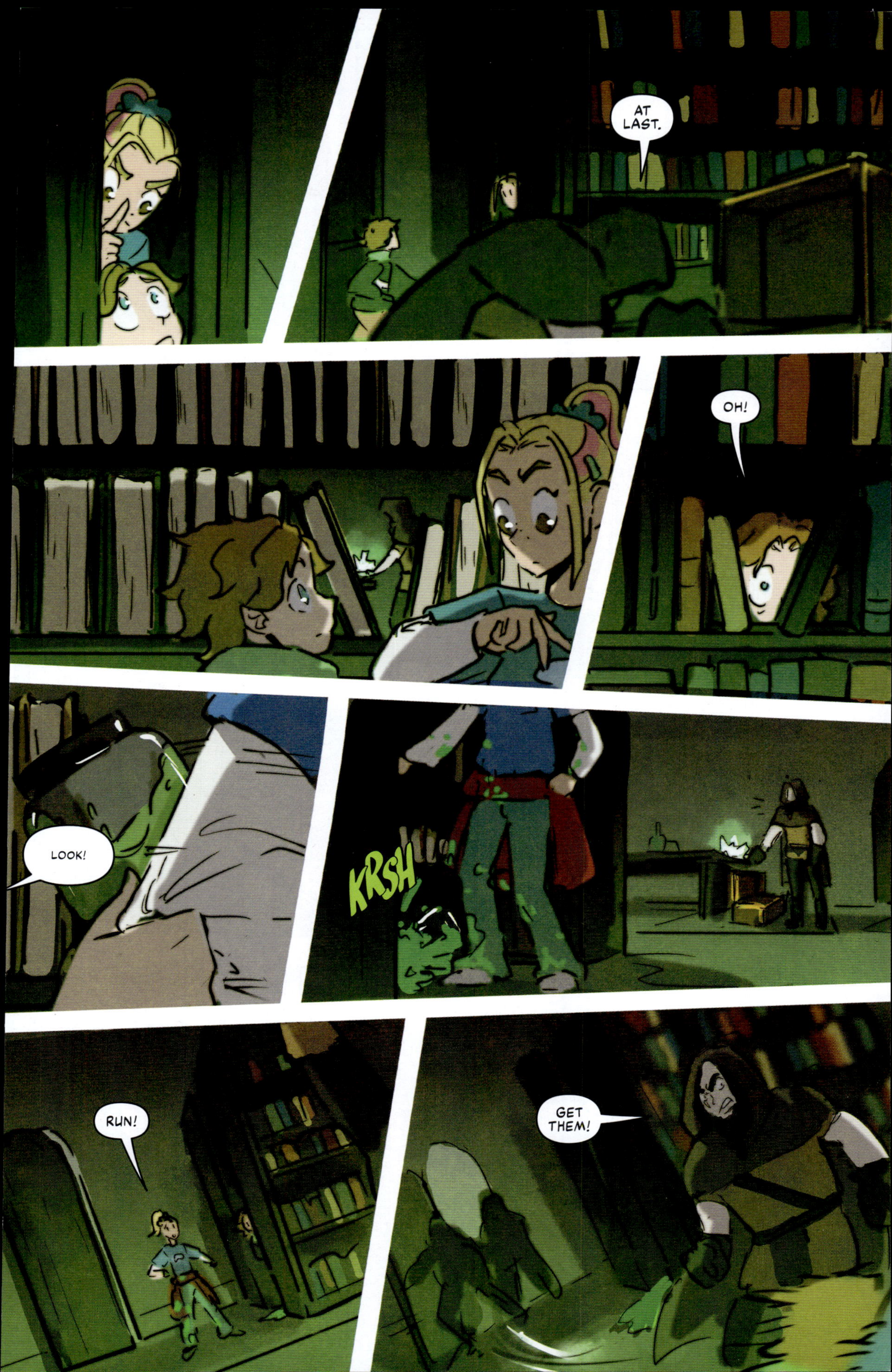
AT LAST.
OH!
LOOK!
KRSH
RUN!
GET THEM!

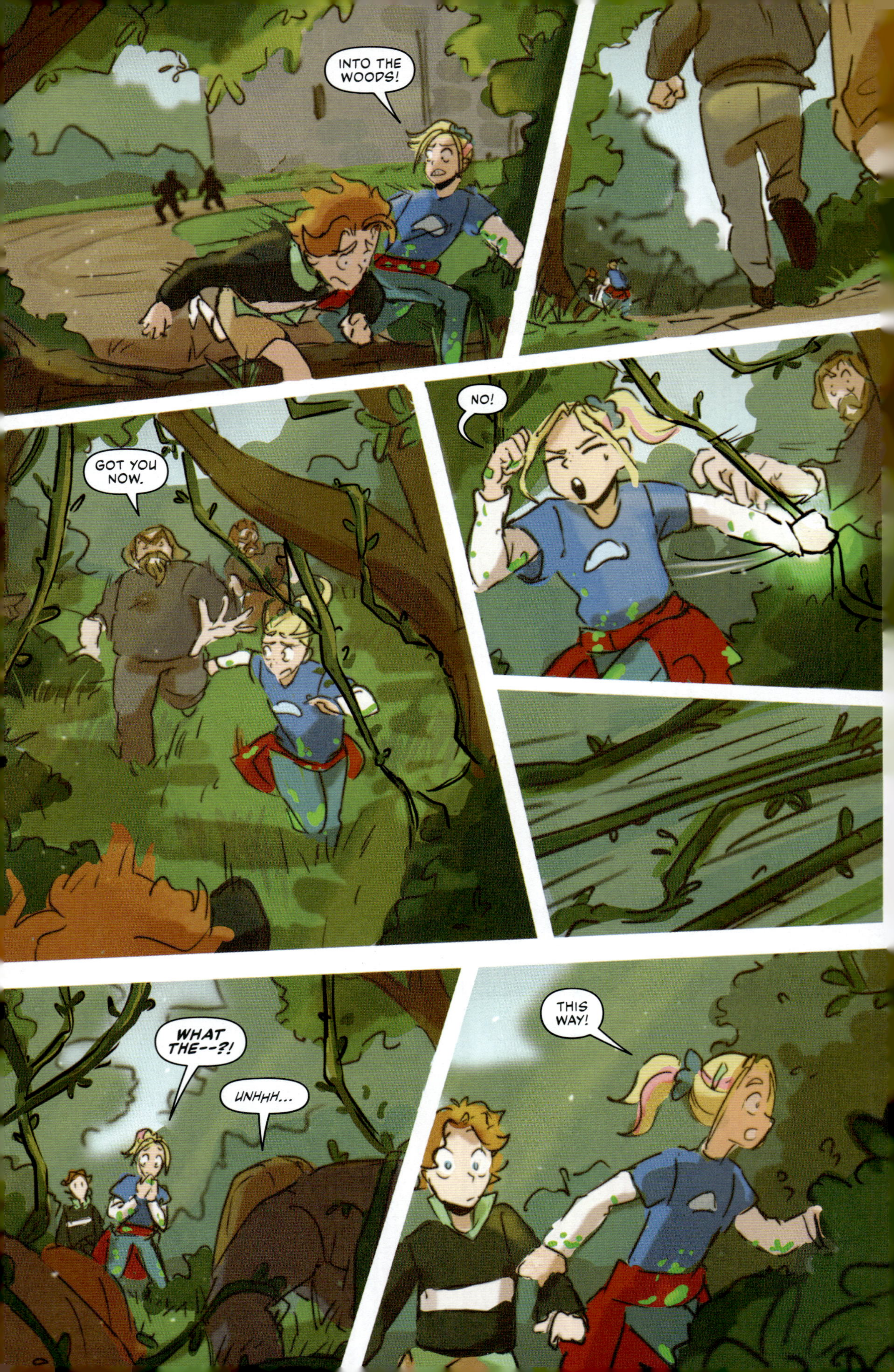
INTO THE WOODS!
GOT YOU NOW.
NO!
WHAT THE--?!
UNHHH...
THIS WAY!

I THINK WE LOST THEM.
WAIT... UP.
EWWW!
IT'S ALL OVER ME!
WHAT IS THIS STUFF?
YOU MADE ME BREAK THAT JAR!
THE CRYSTAL?
I WAS TRYING TO SHOW YOU SOMETHING. CIARAN HAD THE CRYSTAL!
FROM THE HOTEL.
OH, OKAY. I MEAN, YOU'RE SURE IT WASN'T JUST ONE OF THE BILLION OTHER ROCKS ON THIS PLANET?
I'M SURE.

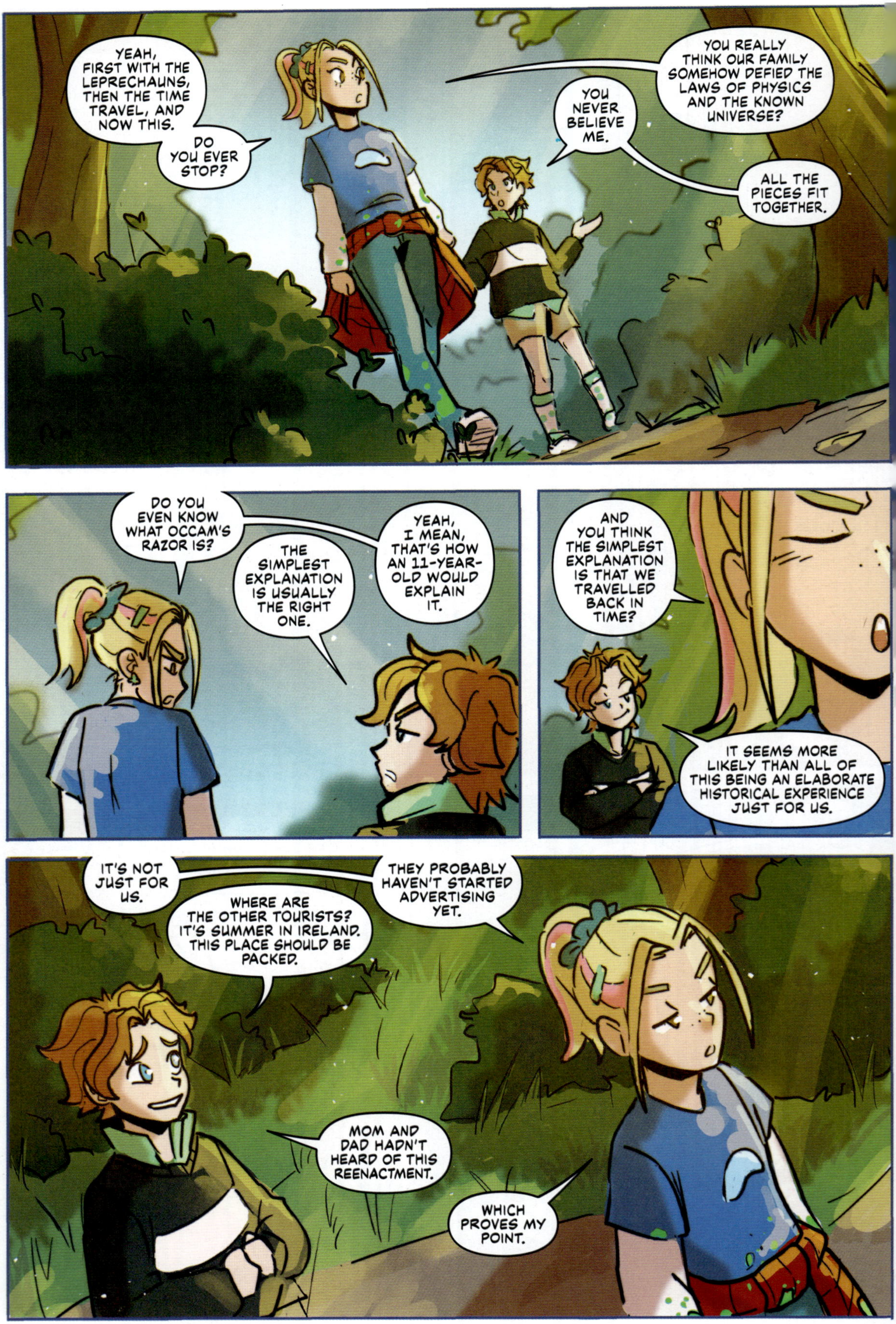
YEAH, FIRST WITH THE LEPRECHAUNS, THEN THE TIME TRAVEL, AND NOW THIS.
DO YOU EVER STOP?
YOU REALLY THINK OUR FAMILY SOMEHOW DEFIED THE LAWS OF PHYSICS AND THE KNOWN UNIVERSE?
YOU NEVER BELIEVE ME.
ALL THE PIECES FIT TOGETHER.
DO YOU EVEN KNOW WHAT OCCAM'S RAZOR IS?
THE SIMPLEST EXPLANATION IS USUALLY THE RIGHT ONE.
YEAH, I MEAN, THAT'S HOW AN 11-YEAR-OLD WOULD EXPLAIN IT.
AND YOU THINK THE SIMPLEST EXPLANATION IS THAT WE TRAVELLED BACK IN TIME?
IT SEEMS MORE LIKELY THAN ALL OF THIS BEING AN ELABORATE HISTORICAL EXPERIENCE JUST FOR US.
IT'S NOT JUST FOR US.
WHERE ARE THE OTHER TOURISTS? IT'S SUMMER IN IRELAND. THIS PLACE SHOULD BE PACKED.
THEY PROBABLY HAVEN'T STARTED ADVERTISING YET.
MOM AND DAD HADN'T HEARD OF THIS REENACTMENT.
WHICH PROVES MY POINT.

YOU'VE GOT TO TRUST ME.
OH, DO YOU SEE ANOTHER FOUR-LEAF CLOVER?
IF THIS GOO MAKES ME SICK--
PLEASE, LILY.
WHAT IF?
OKAY, FINE. LET'S PLAY. WHAT IF THAT REALLY WAS THE CRYSTAL? IT WOULD HAVE EXISTED IN THE PAST, SO IT'S POSSIBLE.
IT WASN'T BROKEN THOUGH.

I GUESS IT WOULDN'T HAVE TO HAVE BEEN. IT JUST NEEDS TO GET SHATTERED SOMETIME BEFORE WE SAW IT.
1,000 YEARS FROM NOW.
SURE.
WE'RE PLAYING "WHAT IF...?" REMEMBER? SO, WHAT IF WE DID TRAVEL BACK IN TIME?
I MEAN... THAT WOULD BE PRETTY COOL.
RIGHT?!
TOTALLY.
BUT THAT WOULD MEAN CIARAN REALLY DOES HAVE MOM AND DAD LOCKED IN A DUNGEON.
AND IT'S UP TO US TO SAVE THEM.

#3 MAIN COVER BY **ASIAH FULMORE**

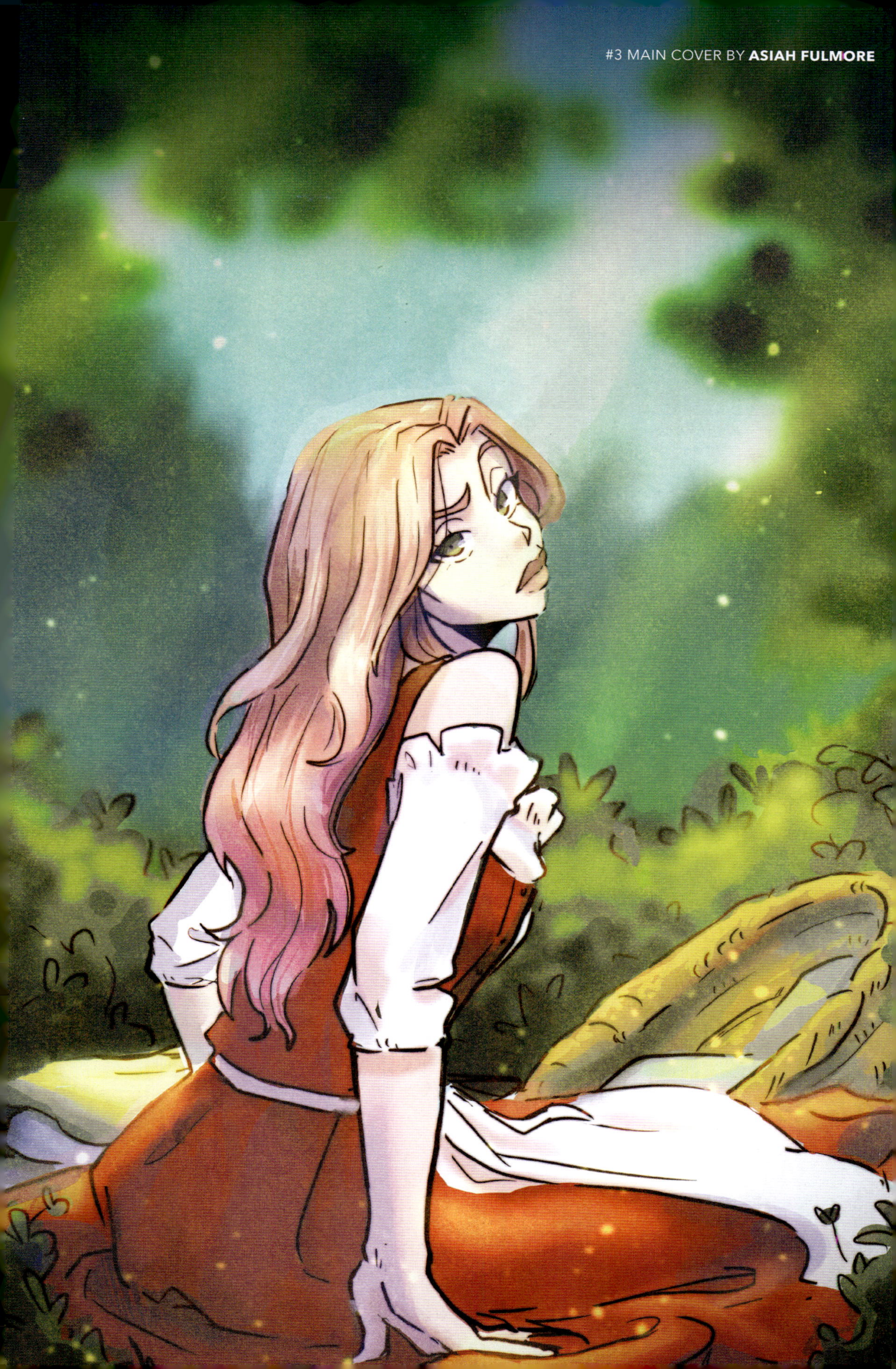

SO, LILY... ANY IDEAS ON HOW WE SNATCH THE DUNGEON KEYS FROM CIARAN AND HIS HENCHMEN?
OUR HOTEL ISN'T FAR FROM HERE. MAYBE THE GUYS THERE CAN HELP.
AND THEN I CAN CHANGE MY CLOTHES, SINCE YOU RUINED THESE, TYLER.
YOUR SUITCASE WAS STILL IN THE LOBBY.
HELLO?
NOK NOK
WOE IS ME! THE SPIRIT VOICES IN MY HEAD ARE BACK AGAIN.
WE'RE NOT VOICES IN YOUR HEAD.
NOK NOK NOK
I THINK ONLY WHATEVER WAS IN OUR ROOM TRAVELED BACK IN TIME WITH US.
GET OUT! GO AWAY!
OPEN THE DOOR.
BAM BAM BAM

FAIR FOLK--FAIRIES--WERE TALES FOR CHILDREN.
RORY, WE'RE REAL. AND WE'RE GUESTS AT YOUR HOTEL.
WHAT'S A HOTEL?
TOLD YOU YOUR SUITCASE ISN'T HERE.
IS THE OLD MAN BACK YET?
OLD MAN?
OH, I SAW HIS NAME ON THE I.D. IN THE CAB. IT'S RORY.

MY NAME IS RORY.
HIS NAME IS RORY.
WHAT A COINCIDENCE.
OH, LAD, THERE ARE NO...
COINCIDENCES IN IRELAND.
...COINCIDENCES IN IRELAND.
WE'VE HEARD IT SOME-WHEN BEFORE.
UGH.
I'M LILY. THIS IS TYLER.

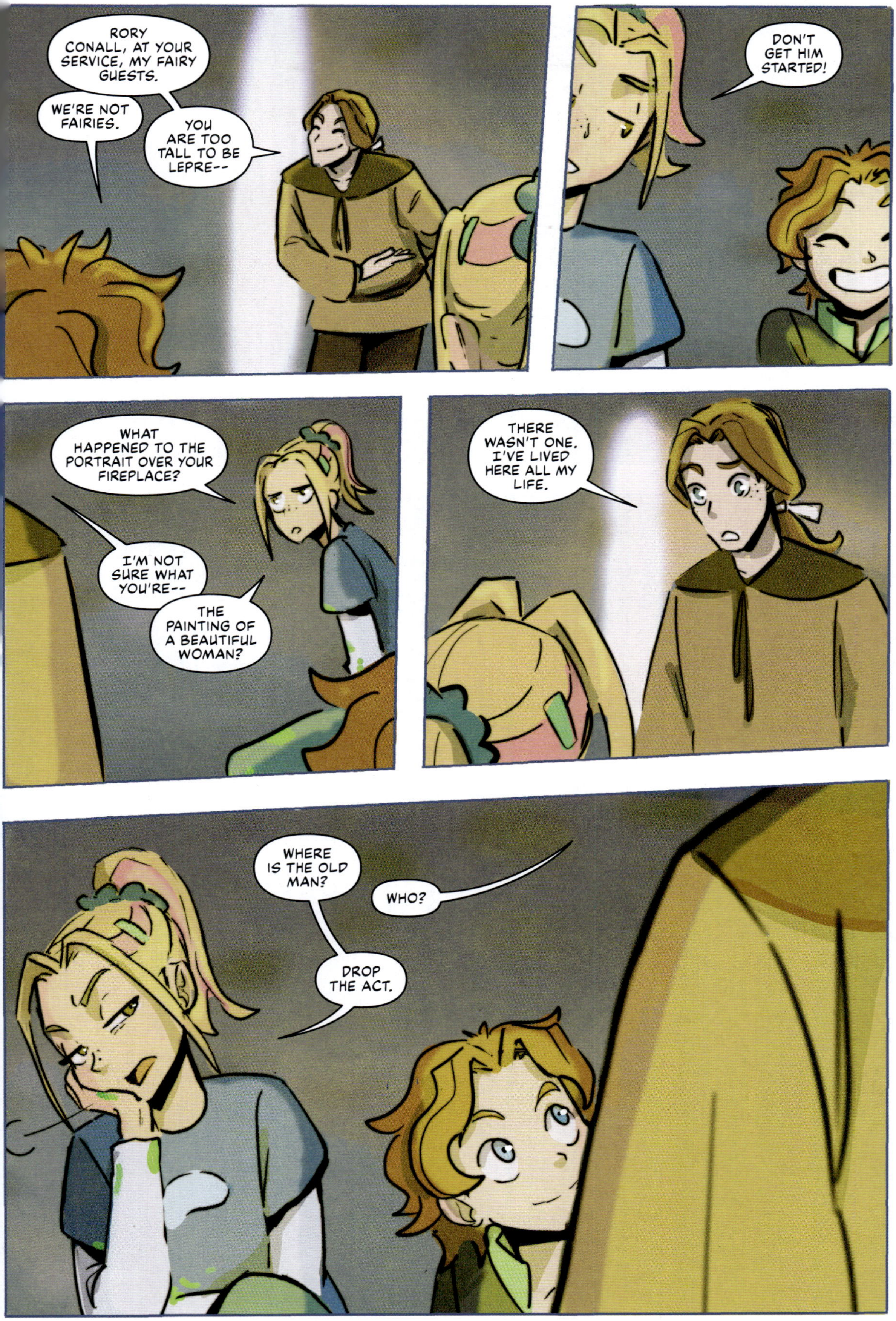
RORY CONALL, AT YOUR SERVICE, MY FAIRY GUESTS.
WE'RE NOT FAIRIES.
YOU ARE TOO TALL TO BE LEPRE--
DON'T GET HIM STARTED!
WHAT HAPPENED TO THE PORTRAIT OVER YOUR FIREPLACE?
I'M NOT SURE WHAT YOU'RE--
THE PAINTING OF A BEAUTIFUL WOMAN?
THERE WASN'T ONE. I'VE LIVED HERE ALL MY LIFE.
WHERE IS THE OLD MAN?
WHO?
DROP THE ACT.

RORY, WHO'S THE BEST BASKETBALL PLAYER OF ALL TIME?
BASKET... BALL?
MINECRAFT OR ROBLOX?
I'M SORRY, I--
WHO'S THE PRESIDENT OF THE UNITED STATES?
THE WHAT?
OH, COME ON.
I REALLY DON'T THINK HE'S ACTING.
AH HA!
HOW DO YOU EXPLAIN THIS?

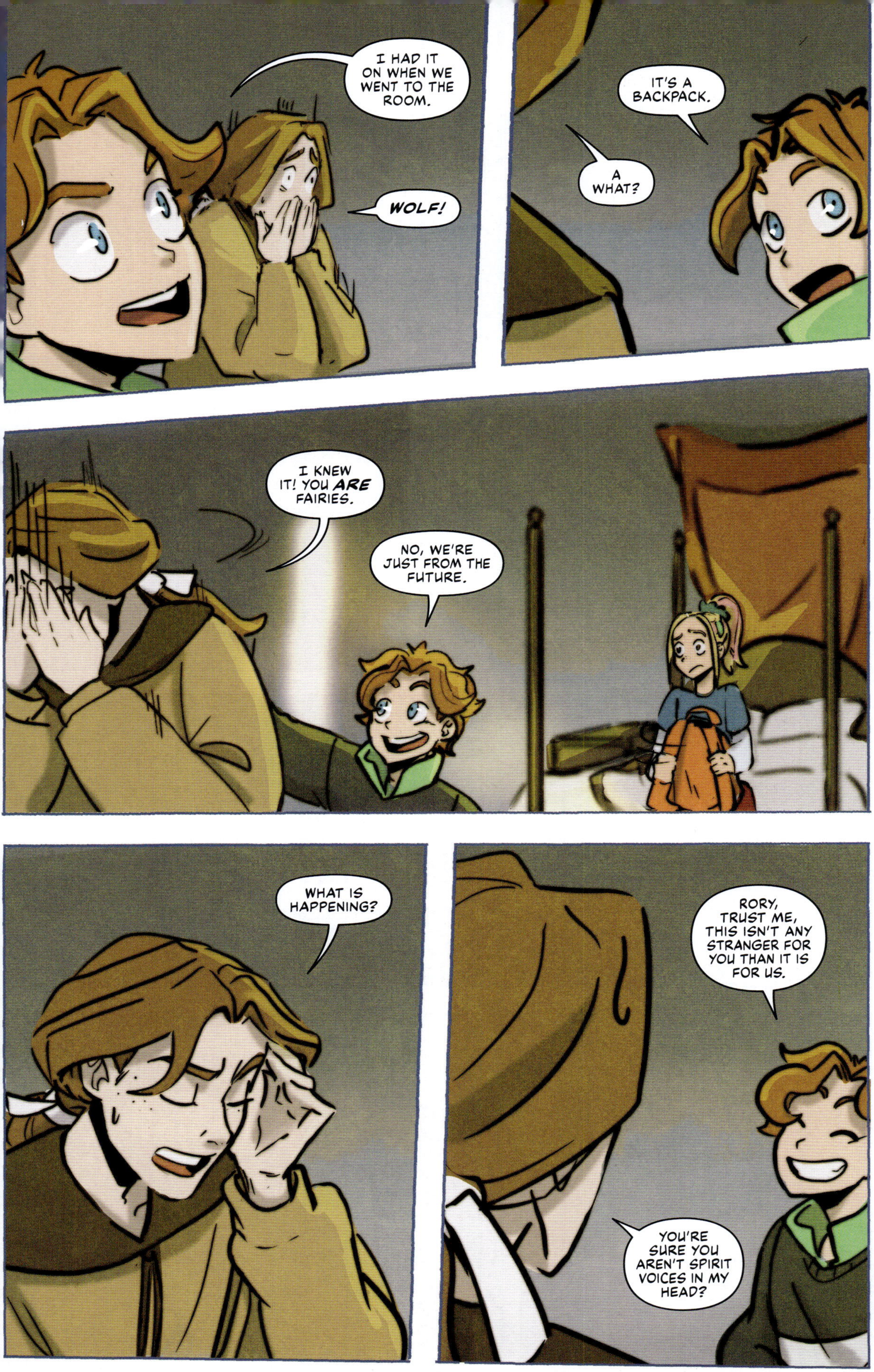
I HAD IT ON WHEN WE WENT TO THE ROOM.
WOLF!
IT'S A BACKPACK.
A WHAT?
I KNEW IT! YOU ARE FAIRIES.
NO, WE'RE JUST FROM THE FUTURE.
WHAT IS HAPPENING?
RORY, TRUST ME, THIS ISN'T ANY STRANGER FOR YOU THAN IT IS FOR US.
YOU'RE SURE YOU AREN'T SPIRIT VOICES IN MY HEAD?

UUUGH...
I SWEAR THERE WAS A LIGHT RIGHT HERE.
THERE WILL BE IN THE FUTURE.
AND THERE'S NO ELECTRICAL WIRING.
OCCAM'S RAZOR.
DON'T THINK THAT I'VE FORGIVEN YOU FOR GETTING THIS SLIME ON ME.
NO KITCHEN. NO BATHROOMS.
RORY'S NEVER EVEN HEARD OF CHOCOLATE. YOU'VE GOT TO TRY IT!
TOO BAD YOU DIDN'T BRING ANY OF MOM'S COOKIES.
I ATE THEM ALL ON THE PLANE!
I'M SURE I'LL BE WAKING UP SOON.
I WISH I KNEW MORE ABOUT ANCIENT IRISH HISTORY, TO PROVE IT TO HIM.
AND ME.
CARS, PHONES, TV... VIDEO GAMES!
THERE WASN'T EVEN RECORDED MUSIC UNTIL THE 1900S.
OH MAN... WHAT DO YOU DO FOR FUN?!
I NEED SOME AIR.
ME TOO.

THE SIGN FOR THE ROYAL COAST CASTLE HOTEL ISN'T OVER HERE ANYMORE.
OHHH, I GET IT. THIS ISN'T A HOTEL YET. THAT'S WHY RORY--OLD RORY--TOLD US YOUNG RORY WOULDN'T BE EXPECTING VISITORS.
CERTAINLY NOT ONES ROM THE FUTURE.
WAIT, HOW WOULD RORY IN THE FUTURE KNOW ABOUT RORY IN THE PAST?
BECAUSE THEY ARE THE SAME PERSON!
THIS IS A LOT TO PROCESS.
RORY, WE NEED YOUR HELP TO RESCUE OUR PARENTS.
AND NOW A QUEST?
HE WOULDN'T EVEN TRY THE CANDY BAR.

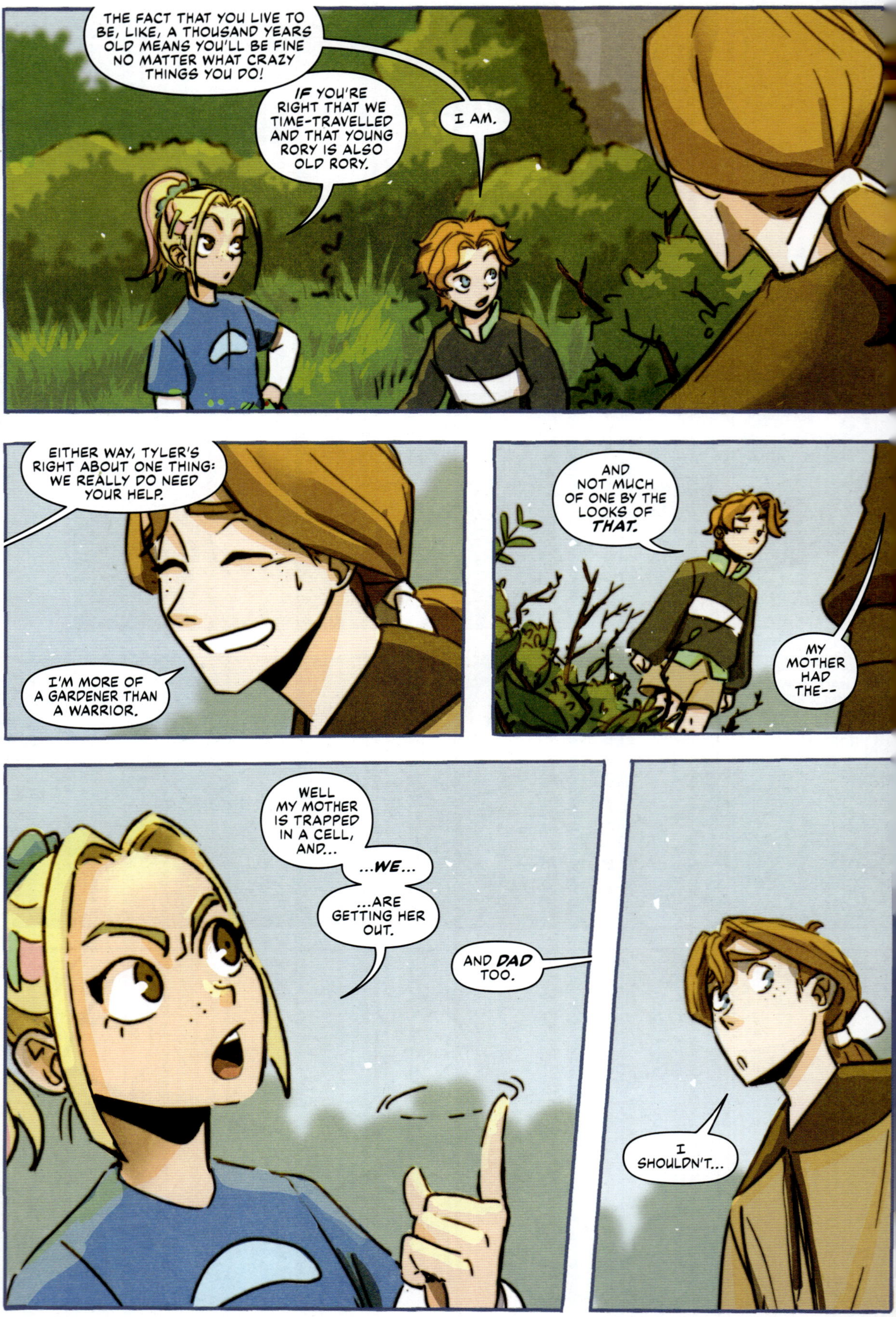
THE FACT THAT YOU LIVE TO BE, LIKE, A THOUSAND YEARS OLD MEANS YOU'LL BE FINE NO MATTER WHAT CRAZY THINGS YOU DO!
IF YOU'RE RIGHT THAT WE TIME-TRAVELLED AND THAT YOUNG RORY IS ALSO OLD RORY.
I AM.
EITHER WAY, TYLER'S RIGHT ABOUT ONE THING: WE REALLY DO NEED YOUR HELP.
I'M MORE OF A GARDENER THAN A WARRIOR.
AND NOT MUCH OF ONE BY THE LOOKS OF THAT.
MY MOTHER HAD THE--
WELL MY MOTHER IS TRAPPED IN A CELL, AND...
...WE...
...ARE GETTING HER OUT.
AND DAD TOO.
I SHOULDN'T...

Panel 1:
- "YOU SHOULD."
- "I'M SORRY. I'M A BIT OF A..."

Panel 2:
- "WE AT LEAST NEED YOUR HELP FINDING OUR WAY BACK."
- "I CAN'T."

Panel 3:
- "WOOOOA!"

Panel 4:
- "YOU CAN'T BECAUSE THAT'S NOT YOUR *ROLE?*"
- "I DON'T KNOW WHAT YOU'RE--"
- "YOU CAN STOP PRETENDING."
- "I'M NOT--"
- "IF TYLER IS RIGHT, MY PARENTS ARE IN *REAL* DANGER!"

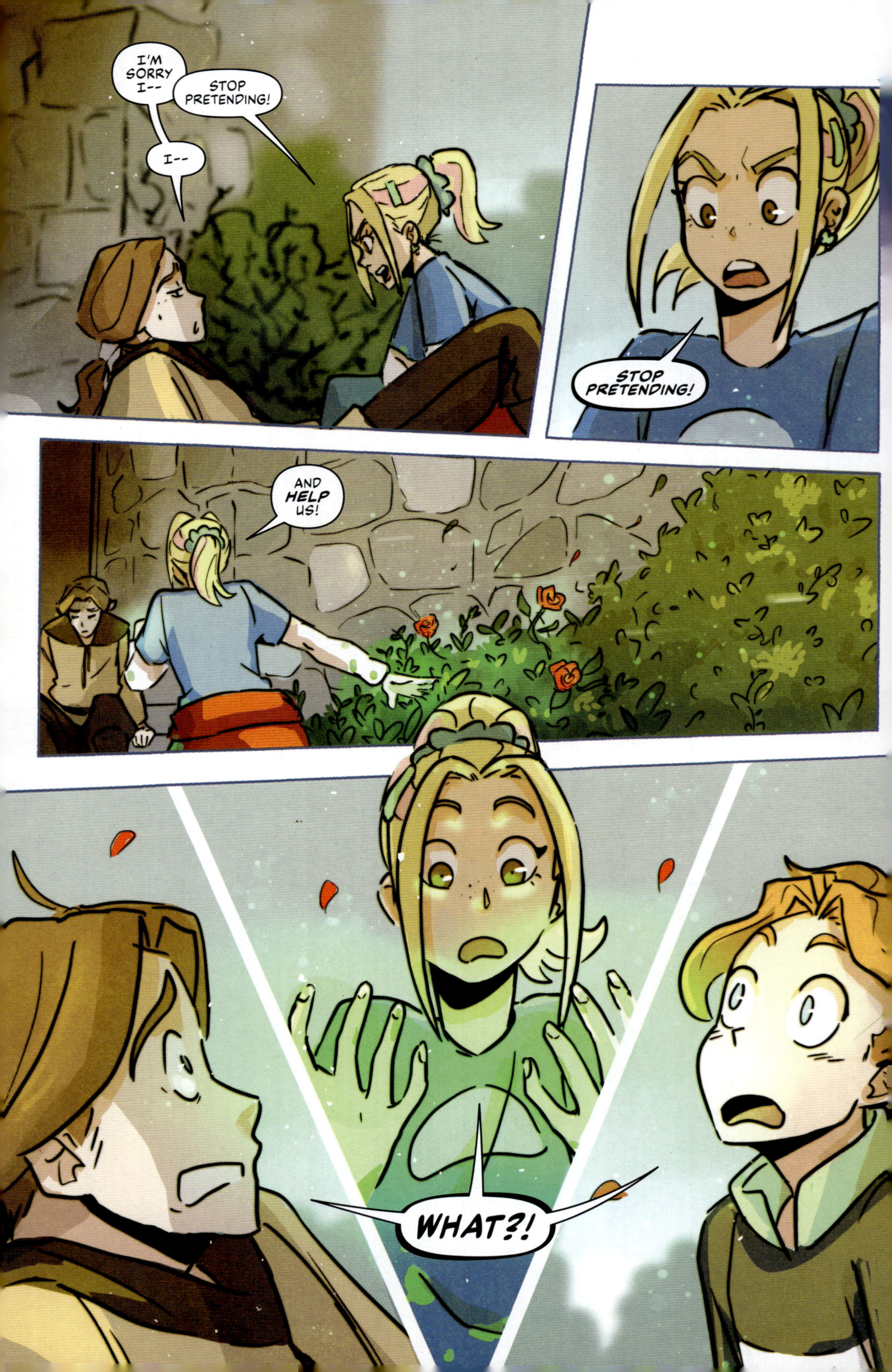
I'M SORRY I--
STOP PRETENDING!
I--
STOP PRETENDING!
AND HELP US!
WHAT?!

IN THE WOODS, I THOUGHT I SAW--
I KNEW YOU WERE FAIRIES!
WE'RE NOT--
DO YOU THINK TIME TRAVEL GAVE US SUPERPOWERS?!
SUPER SPEED!
NOPE!
SUPER STRENGTH!
NOPE!
AWWW, MAN!
I WAS BEGINNING TO THINK YOU WERE MAKE-BELIEVE.
OH, I'M REAL.
REAL CONFUSED.
THE LEGENDS ARE TRUE!
SO, AREN'T YOU, LIKE, SUPPOSED TO HONOR AND WORSHIP HER?
AND DO ANYTHING I SAY?

SO... NATURE POWERS, *HUH?*
I'VE ALWAYS BEEN GOOD AT PUZZLES. MAYBE THAT'S SOMETHING?
HAVE YOU ALWAYS HAD THE GIFT?
THIS IS A ***VERY*** NEW THING.
IN COMIC BOOKS...
...*UH,* THAT'S BOOKS WITH DRAWINGS USUALLY ABOUT PEOPLE WITH SPECIAL POWERS... ANYWAY, IN COMIC BOOKS, A LOT OF MUTANTS DON'T GET THEIR POWERS TILL PUBERTY.
'TIL THEY'RE AROUND THIRTEEN YEARS OLD? LIKE ME.
BUT I DON'T THINK YOU'RE A MUTANT.
IT WAS OBVIOUSLY THE GREEN GOO.
GEE... THANKS.
YOU ***THINK?***
YOU'RE WELCOME, BY THE WAY.
WHAT IF IT WAS POISON OR RADIOACTIVE OR--
GAMMA RAYS, SPIDER BITES, MAGICAL ARTIFACTS... IT ALWAYS TURNS OUT FINE IN COMICS.
THAT'S NOT COMFORTING.
IT'S TOO BAD YOU DON'T EVEN WATCH SUPERHERO MOVIES.
NOT MY THING.
WELL, THEN AT LEAST YOU'D KNOW THAT POWERS CAN BE UNLOCKED WHEN SOMEONE IS MEGA-EMOTIONAL OR IN DANGER.
LIKE WHEN THOSE GUYS WERE CHASING US?
GUYS?

THAT *IS* WHEN IT STARTED.
SO NOW YOU JUST NEED TO PRACTICE FOR YEARS TO HONE YOUR SKILLS.
WE DON'T HAVE YEARS, DO WE? HOW CAN I LEARN *NOW?*
WE DON'T HAVE TIME TO GO FISHING!
YOU HAVE TO PUT THE TROUT IN THE NET BEFORE YOU PUT IT IN THE POT.
WELL, THEN YOU BETTER GET SUPER GOOD AT FOCUSING YOUR EMOTIONS, FAST.
FINE. I'LL GIVE IT A TRY.
CONCENTRATE.
SHH!

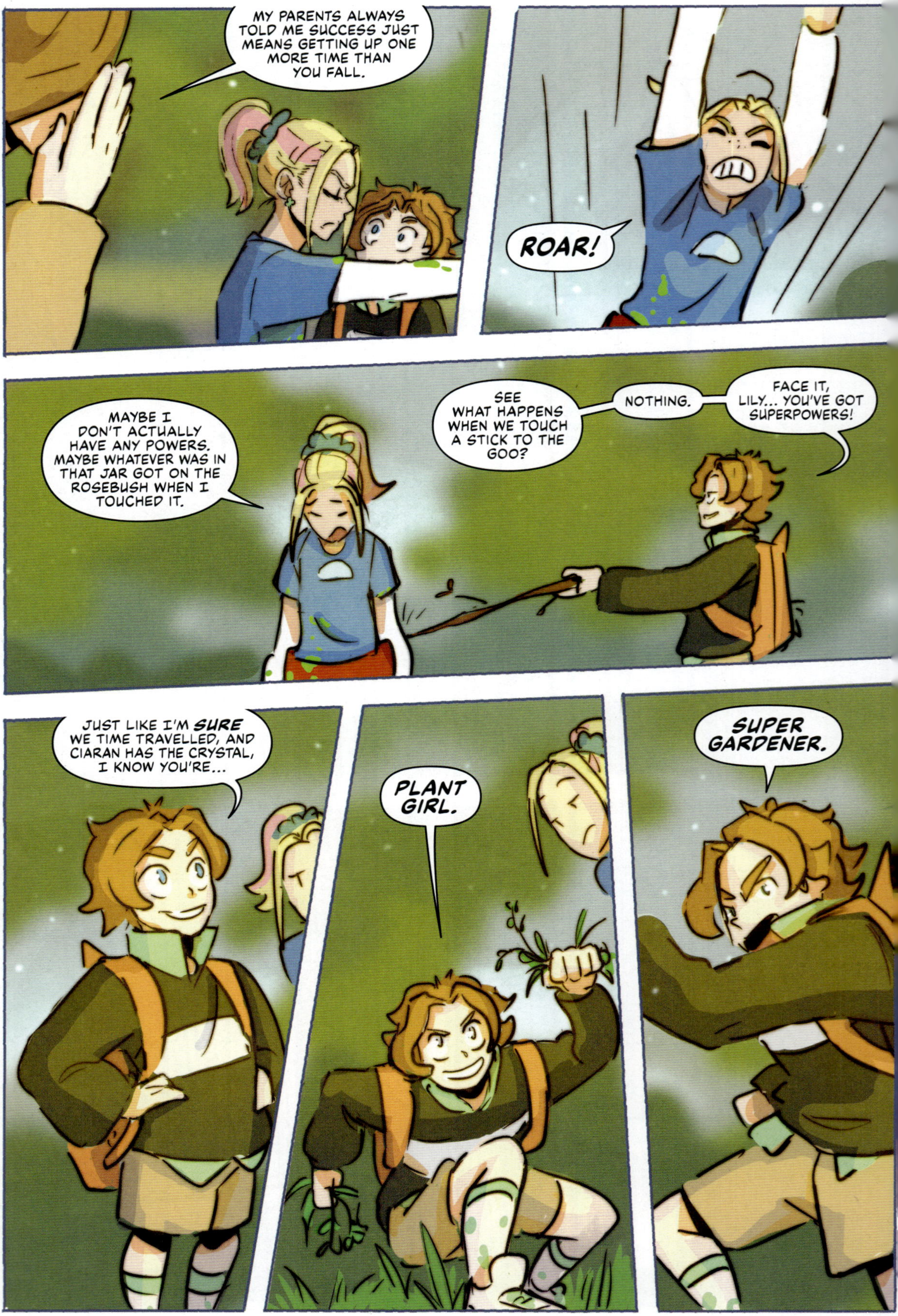
MY PARENTS ALWAYS TOLD ME SUCCESS JUST MEANS GETTING UP ONE MORE TIME THAN YOU FALL.
ROAR!
MAYBE I DON'T ACTUALLY HAVE ANY POWERS. MAYBE WHATEVER WAS IN THAT JAR GOT ON THE ROSEBUSH WHEN I TOUCHED IT.
SEE WHAT HAPPENS WHEN WE TOUCH A STICK TO THE GOO?
NOTHING.
FACE IT, LILY... YOU'VE GOT SUPERPOWERS!
JUST LIKE I'M *SURE* WE TIME TRAVELLED, AND CIARAN HAS THE CRYSTAL, I KNOW YOU'RE...
PLANT GIRL.
SUPER GARDENER.

THE GREEN AVENGER?
NO.
BLOOM.
OOH, THAT'S GOOD!
BUT I SWEAR, IF THAT SLIME GAVE ME SOME KIND OF DISEASE, I'M GIVING IT TO YOU TOO.
WHAT A LOVELY PUB!
INTO THE BRUSH!
LILY... YOUR HAND!
BEST MEAD I'VE EVER HAD.
YOU'RE FLUTHERED.
YOU DID IT AGAIN!
I TOLD YOU YOU COULD DO IT!
I'M AN EXPERT IN THESE THINGS. TRUST ME!

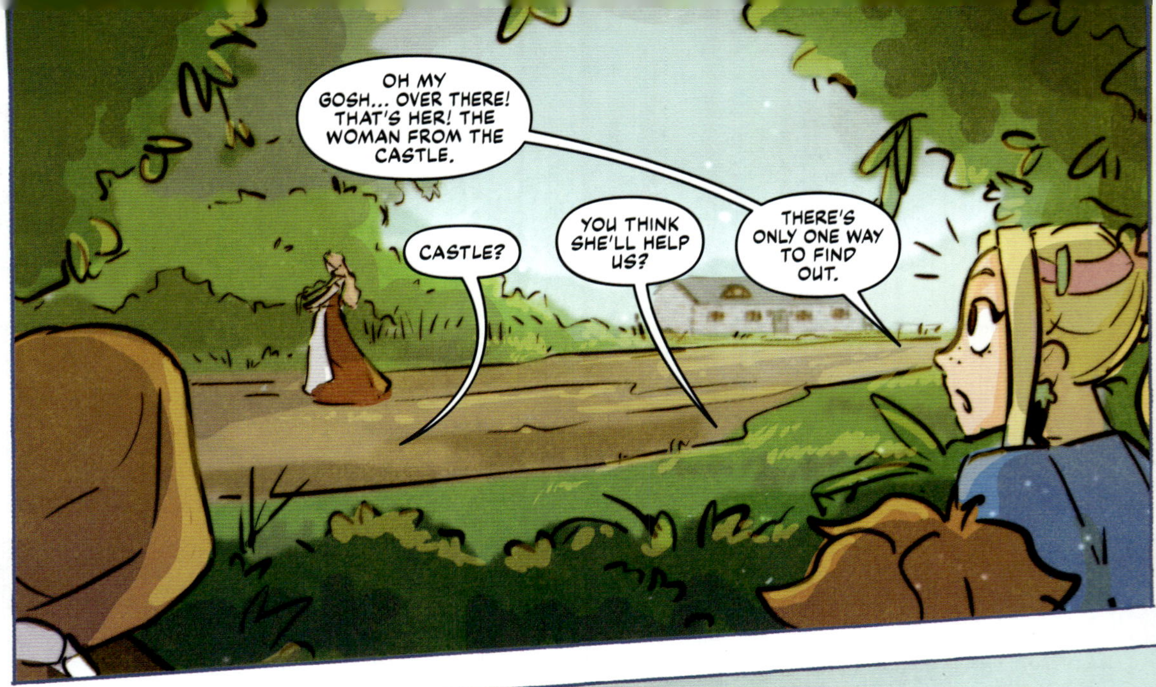
OH MY GOSH... OVER THERE! THAT'S HER! THE WOMAN FROM THE CASTLE.
CASTLE?
YOU THINK SHE'LL HELP US?
THERE'S ONLY ONE WAY TO FIND OUT.

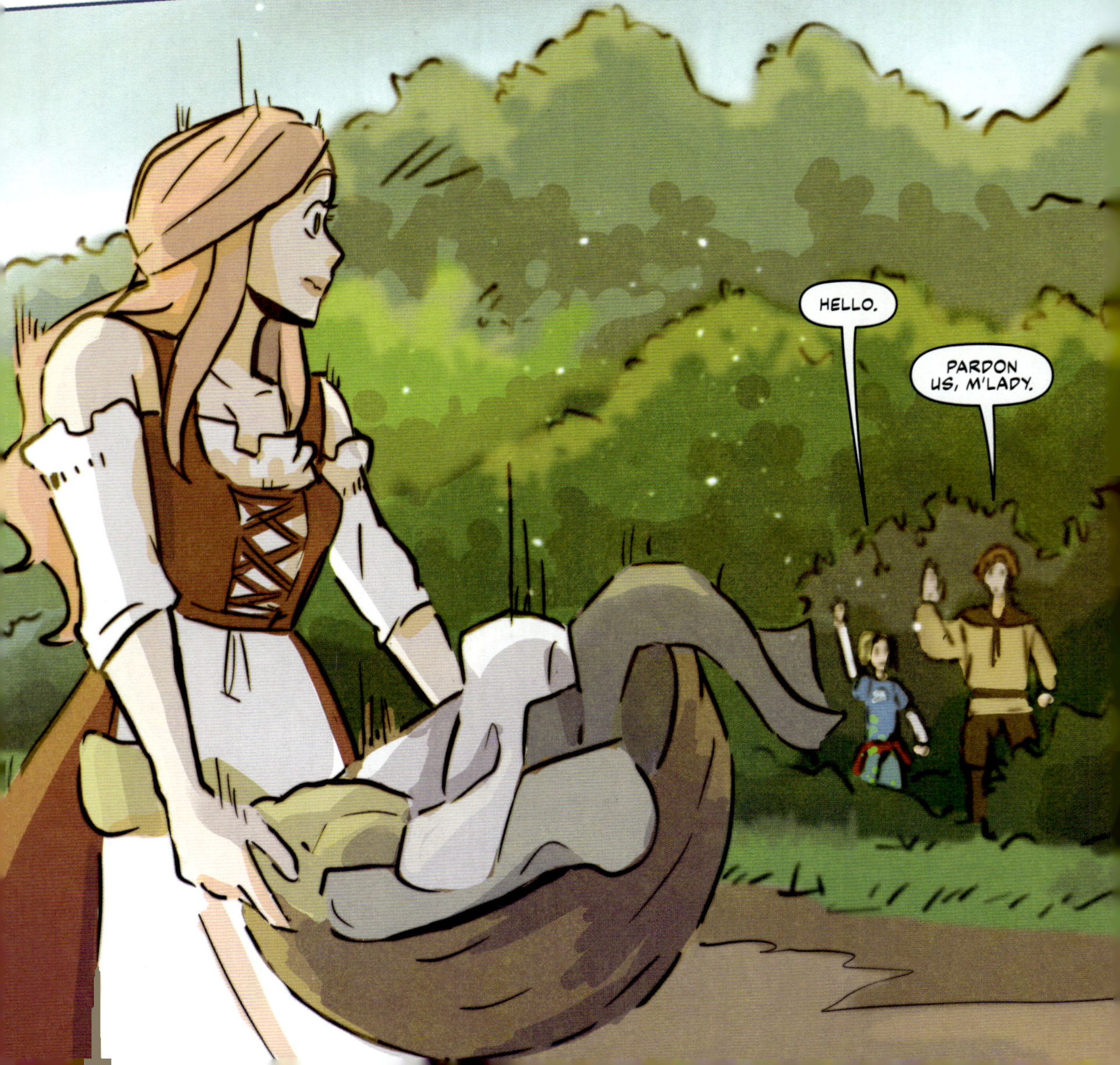
HELLO.
PARDON US, M'LADY.

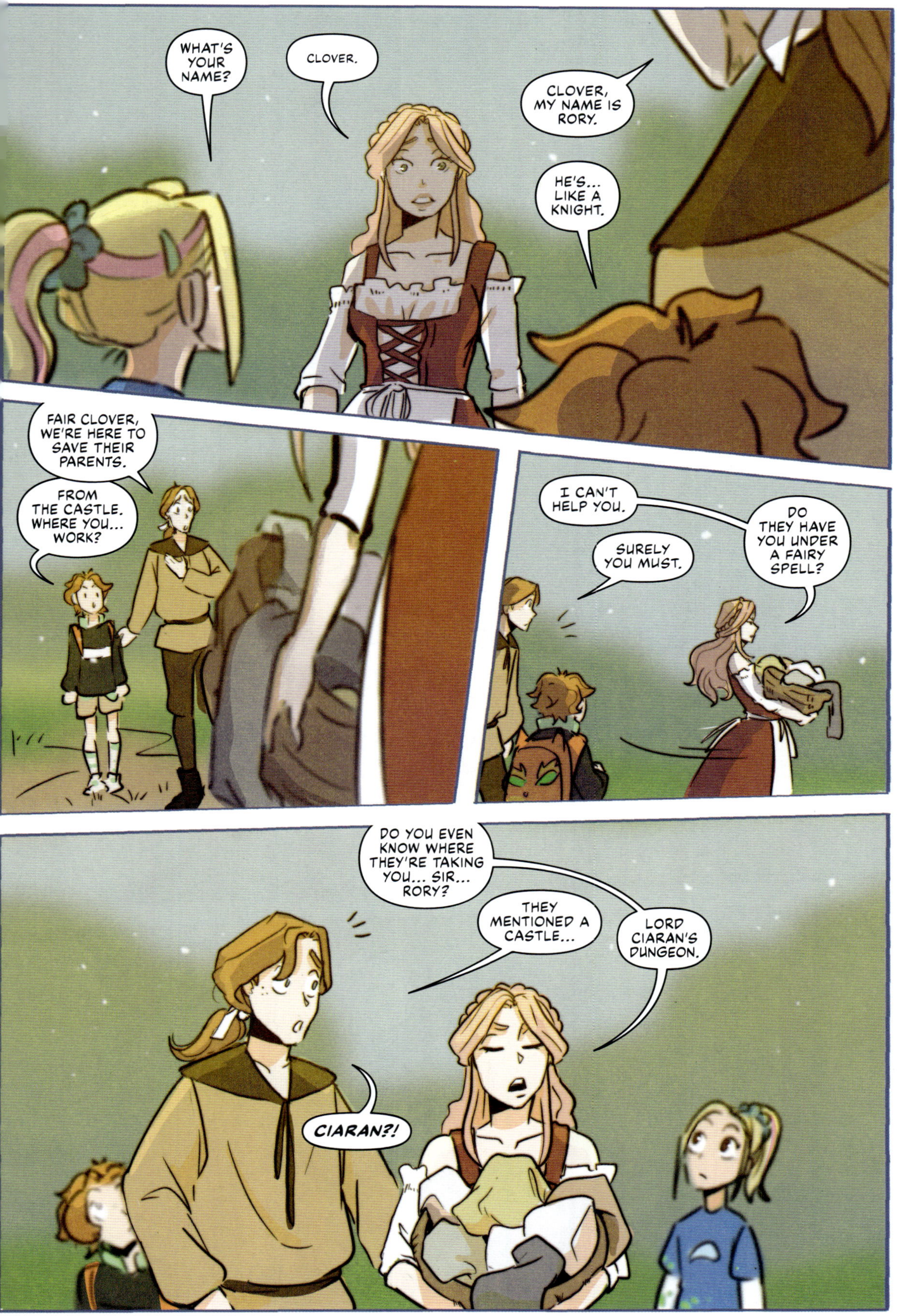
WHAT'S YOUR NAME?
CLOVER.
CLOVER, MY NAME IS RORY.
HE'S... LIKE A KNIGHT.
FAIR CLOVER, WE'RE HERE TO SAVE THEIR PARENTS.
FROM THE CASTLE. WHERE YOU... WORK?
I CAN'T HELP YOU.
DO THEY HAVE YOU UNDER A FAIRY SPELL?
SURELY YOU MUST.
DO YOU EVEN KNOW WHERE THEY'RE TAKING YOU... SIR... RORY?
THEY MENTIONED A CASTLE...
LORD CIARAN'S DUNGEON.
CIARAN?!

YOU DIDN'T TELL ME CIARAN WAS HOLDING YOUR PARENTS.
A BRAVE KNIGHT LIKE YOU. SURELY, YOU CAN'T BE SCARED OF LITTLE OL' ***DR. McSCRUFFLE-FINGERS?***
HE'S THE IRON FIST. THE CLAW.
THAT ONE SUFFERS FROM A DOUBLE-DOSE OF ORIGINAL SIN.
AND YOU WORK FOR HIM?
YOU THINK IT'S A CHOICE?
THEN DON'T YOU WANT TO BE FREE?
THAT WILL NEVER BE AN OPTION FOR ME.

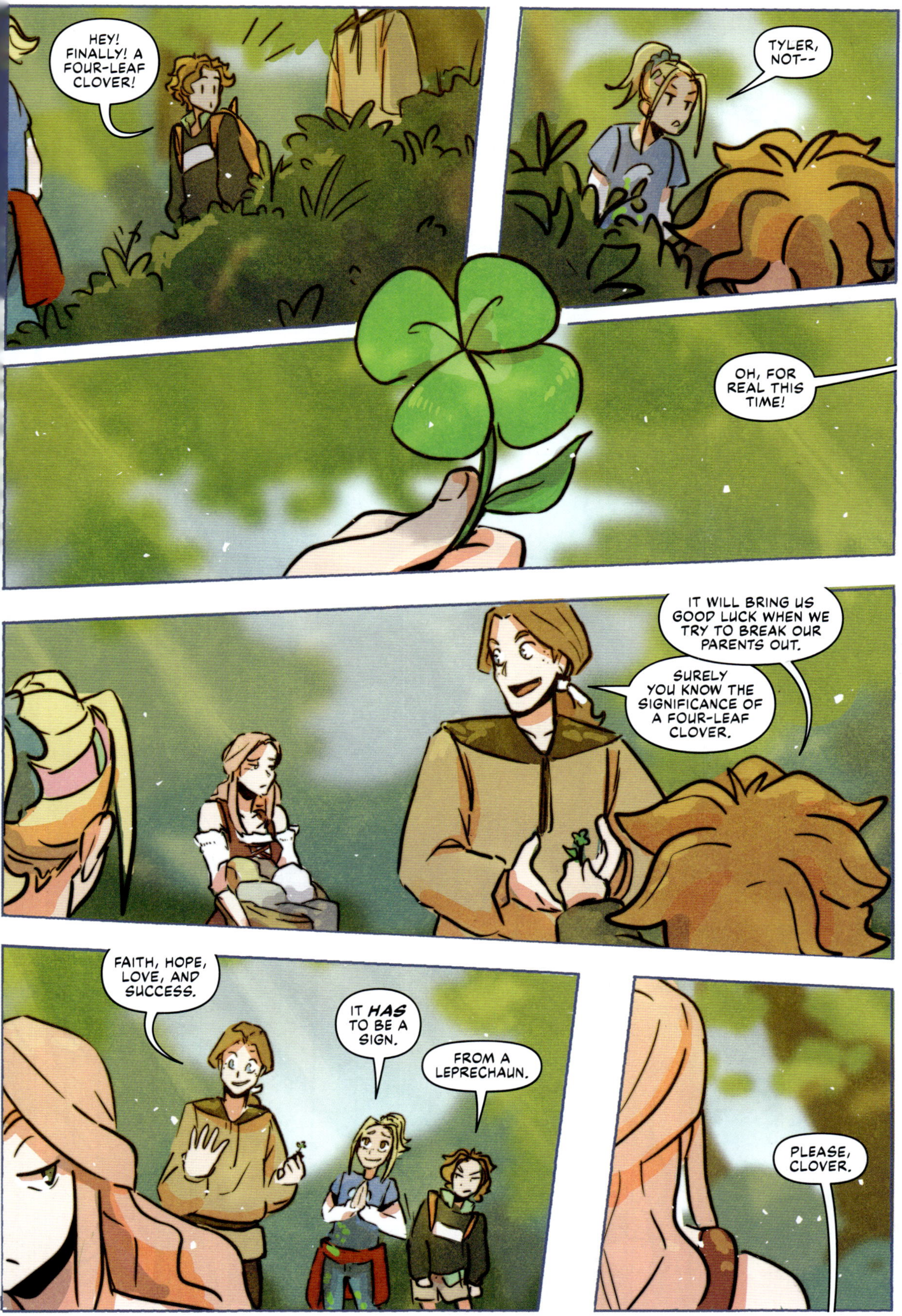
HEY! FINALLY! A FOUR-LEAF CLOVER!
TYLER, NOT--
OH, FOR REAL THIS TIME!
IT WILL BRING US GOOD LUCK WHEN WE TRY TO BREAK OUR PARENTS OUT.
SURELY YOU KNOW THE SIGNIFICANCE OF A FOUR-LEAF CLOVER.
FAITH, HOPE, LOVE, AND SUCCESS.
IT *HAS* TO BE A SIGN.
FROM A LEPRECHAUN.
PLEASE, CLOVER.

HOPE... LEADS TO MISERY.
HOPE IS THE CURE FOR IT AS WELL.
BUT NONE OF YOU ARE DOCTORS.
WELL...
...WHAT ARE YOU WAITING FOR?
SO YOU'VE BEEN CIARAN'S MAID SINCE YOU WERE LITTLE?
SHE'S AN INDENTURED SERVANT.
OH, SO YOU BELIEVE ME NOW.
WELL... THAT'S A BIG CASTLE TO CLEAN ALL BY YOURSELF.
AND SHE HAS TO DO THE LAUNDRY AND COOK TOO.
WHAT? I'M JUST SAYING. WHEN DO CHILD LABOR LAWS GET INVENTED?

WE CAN'T ALL BE BORN HIGH AND MIGHTY.
HEY, NOT ME EITHER.
OH, YES, SIR RORY?
THE TITLE IS... QUITE NEW.
AND WHAT WERE YOU BEFORE THAT, THEN?
I TEND TO SPEND A LOT OF TIME WITH MY OWN THOUGHTS.
WELL, THINKING WON'T DO THE PLOUGHING FOR YOU.
YOU KNOW... RORY IS A BIT OF A CHEF TOO.
REALLY?
YES?
WHY DON'T YOU GIVE HER THE CANDY BAR YOU MADE.
YES!
IT LOOKS LIKE--
TRY IT. IT'S GREAT!
HEHE. JUST SMELL IT.

WHAT IN THE HEAVENS...
RORY'S A WIZARD IN THE KITCHEN, RIGHT?
I'VE NEVER TASTED SOMETHING SO AMAZING IN ALL MY LIFE.
YOU SHOULD TRY ONE OF MY MOM'S COOKIES, THEN.
COOKIE?
THERE AREN'T EVEN COOKIES YET?!
THANK YOU, SIR RORY.
SO WHAT'S THE PLAN?
THERE'S ONLY ONE WAY IN AND ONE WAY OUT.

THOSE TWO GUARDS DON'T LOOK VERY INVITING.
LEAVE THEM TO ME. BUT ONCE I GET YOU IN, YOU'RE ON YOUR OWN.
WITH YOUR HELP, WE CAN ALL BE FREE.
NO MATTER WHAT HAPPENS, CLOVER, THANK YOU FOR SHORTENING OUR ROAD TODAY.
LET'S GO!
WAIT!

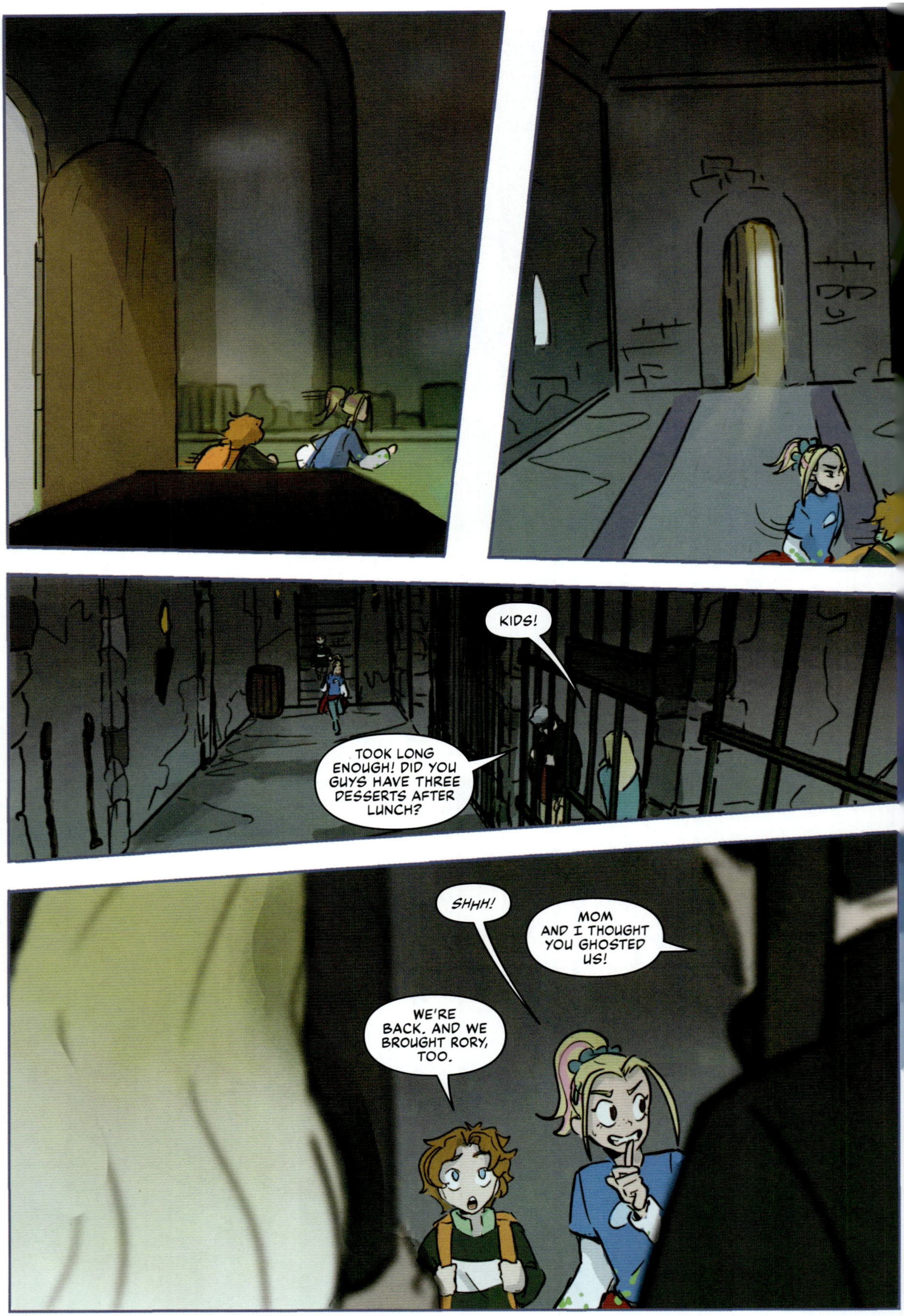
KIDS!
TOOK LONG ENOUGH! DID YOU GUYS HAVE THREE DESSERTS AFTER LUNCH?
SHHH!
MOM AND I THOUGHT YOU GHOSTED US!
WE'RE BACK. AND WE BROUGHT RORY, TOO.

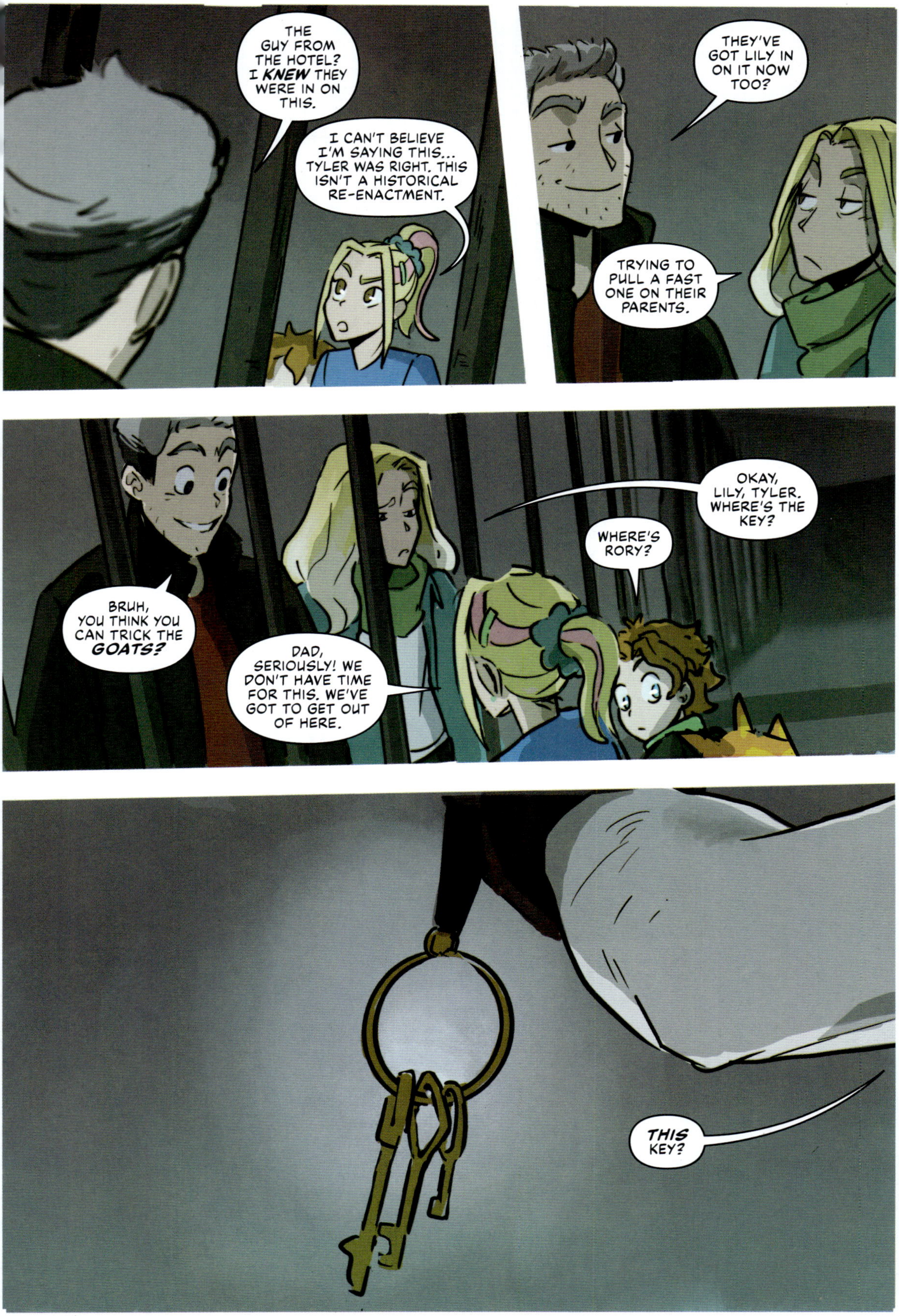
THE GUY FROM THE HOTEL? I **KNEW** THEY WERE IN ON THIS.
I CAN'T BELIEVE I'M SAYING THIS... TYLER WAS RIGHT. THIS ISN'T A HISTORICAL RE-ENACTMENT.
THEY'VE GOT LILY IN ON IT NOW TOO?
TRYING TO PULL A FAST ONE ON THEIR PARENTS.
OKAY, LILY, TYLER. WHERE'S THE KEY?
BRUH, YOU THINK YOU CAN TRICK THE ***GOATS?***
DAD, SERIOUSLY! WE DON'T HAVE TIME FOR THIS. WE'VE GOT TO GET OUT OF HERE.
WHERE'S RORY?
THIS KEY?

#4 MAIN COVER BY **ASIAH FULMORE**

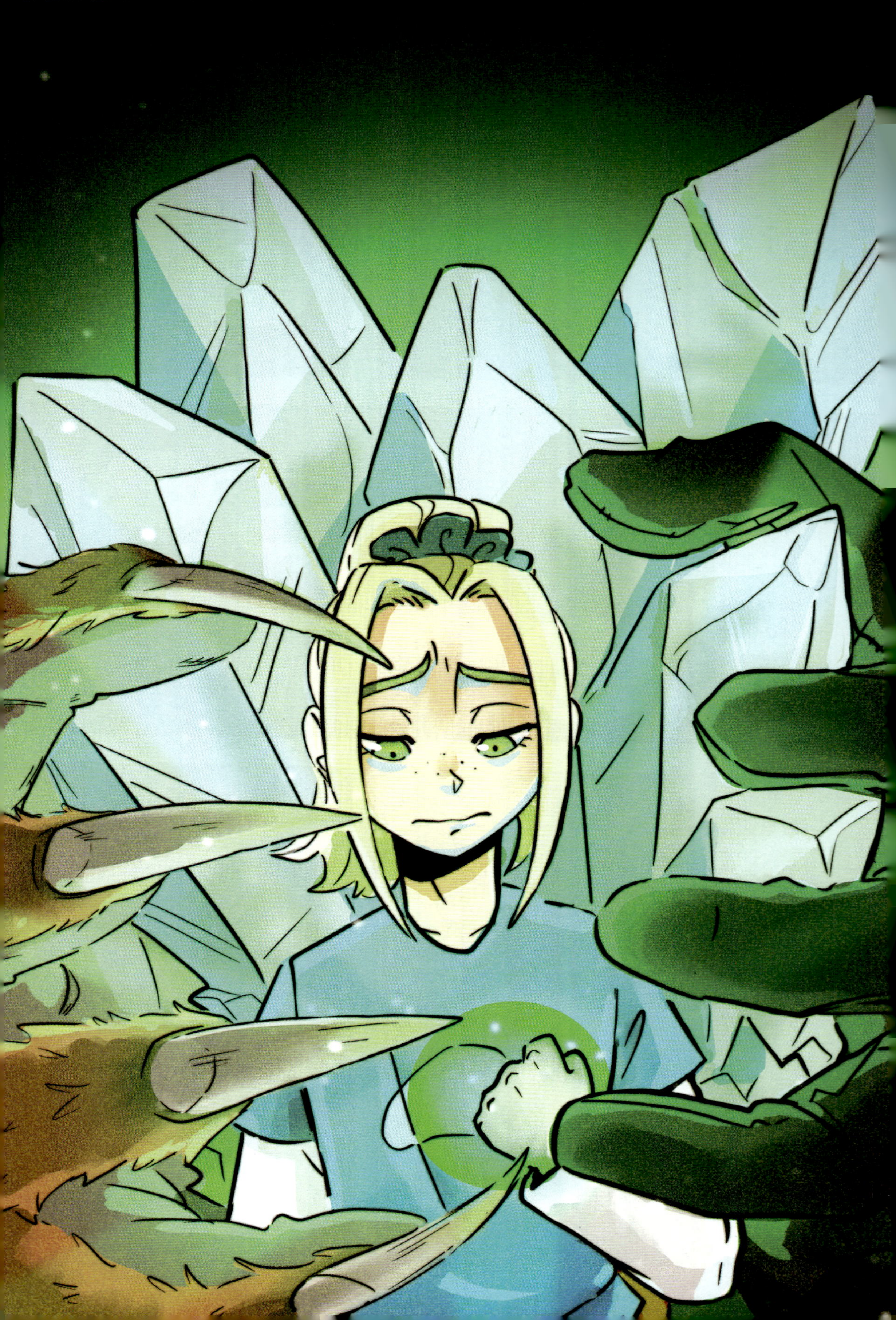

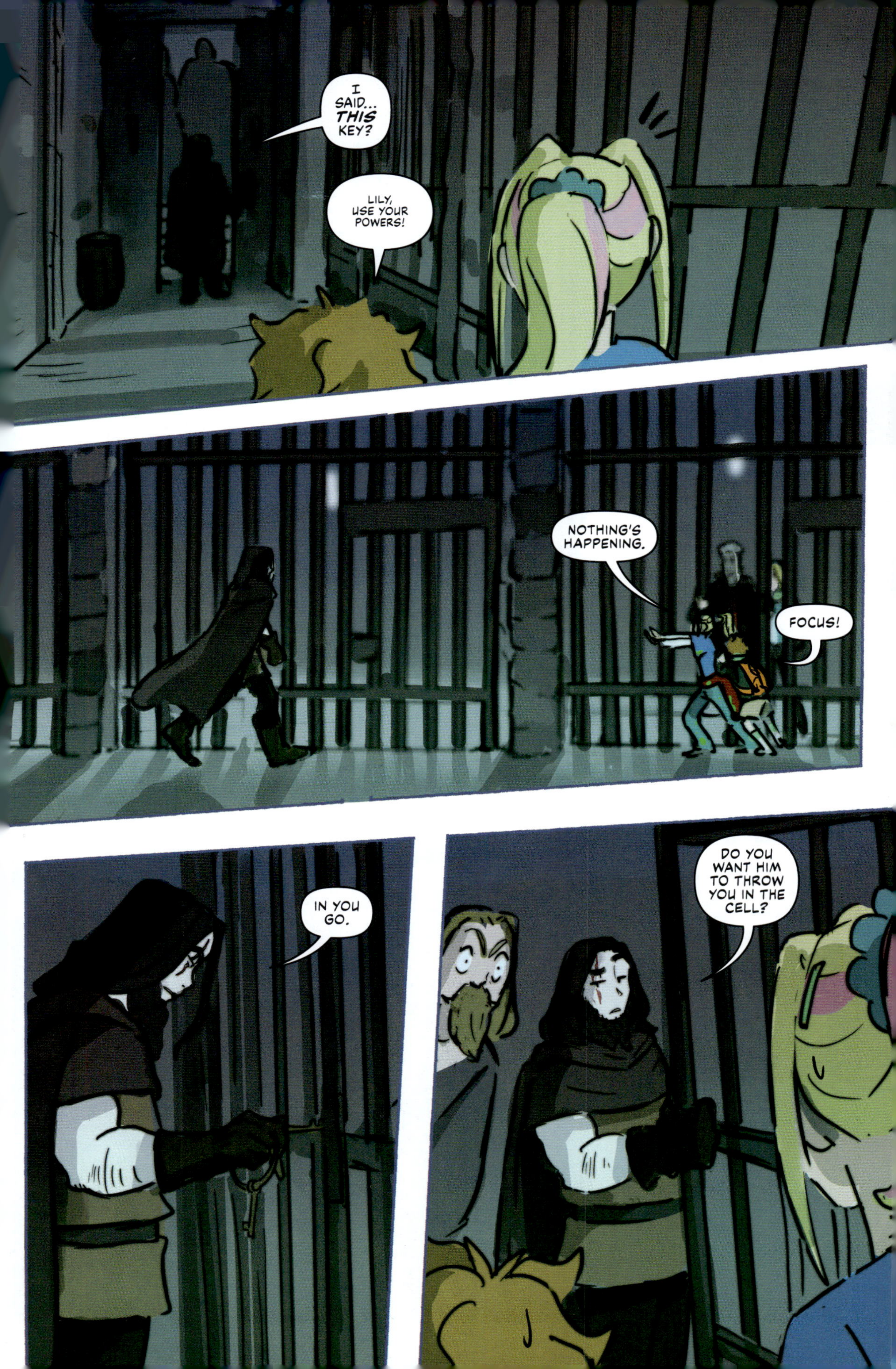
I SAID... *THIS* KEY?
LILY, USE YOUR POWERS!
NOTHING'S HAPPENING.
FOCUS!
IN YOU GO.
DO YOU WANT HIM TO THROW YOU IN THE CELL?

KLIK
YOU'RE REALLY GOING TO MAKE THEM SQUEEZE THROUGH THE BARS AGAIN?
THE WRITERS OF THIS SHOULD TRY ONE OF THOSE ESCAPE ROOMS.
CREEEAK
ALL RIGHT! THAT'S MORE LIKE IT.
NOW WE'LL NEED TO FIGURE OUT A NEW WAY TO BREAK OUT.
EXCITING!

I HEAR YOU HAVE A GREEN THUMB?
THAT SOUNDS LIKE A CLUE.
ACTUALLY, I'M GETTING PRETTY HUNGRY. AND LAUREN IS FREEZING.
THIS HAS BEEN A LOT OF FUN, BUT SHOW'S OVER. IT'S TIME TO LET US OUT.
grrrgle
LET YOU OUT?
NO.
I HAVE OTHER PLANS FOR YOU.

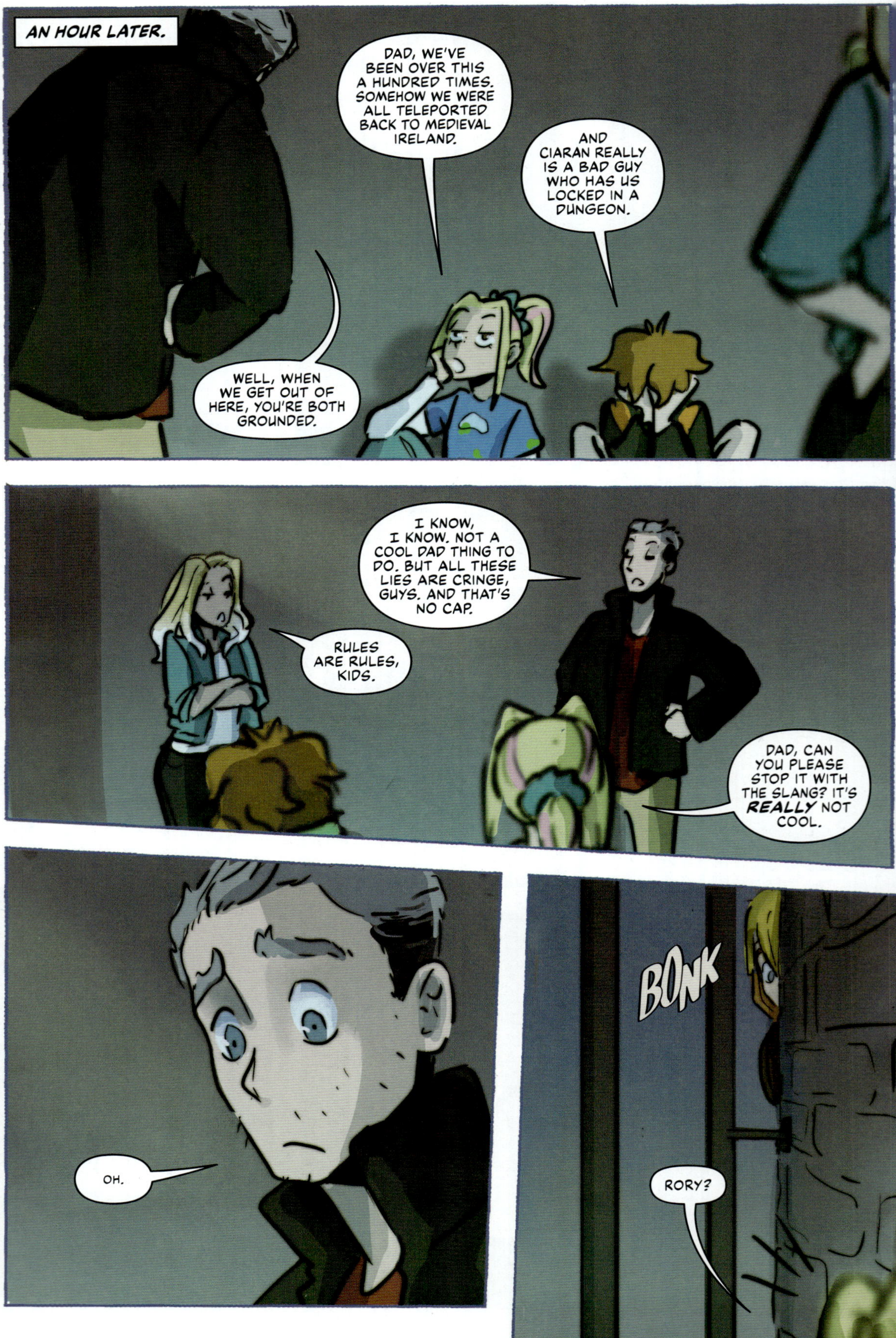
AN HOUR LATER.
DAD, WE'VE BEEN OVER THIS A HUNDRED TIMES. SOMEHOW WE WERE ALL TELEPORTED BACK TO MEDIEVAL IRELAND.
AND CIARAN REALLY IS A BAD GUY WHO HAS US LOCKED IN A DUNGEON.
WELL, WHEN WE GET OUT OF HERE, YOU'RE BOTH GROUNDED.
I KNOW, I KNOW. NOT A COOL DAD THING TO DO. BUT ALL THESE LIES ARE CRINGE, GUYS. AND THAT'S NO CAP.
RULES ARE RULES, KIDS.
DAD, CAN YOU PLEASE STOP IT WITH THE SLANG? IT'S REALLY NOT COOL.
OH.
BONK
RORY?

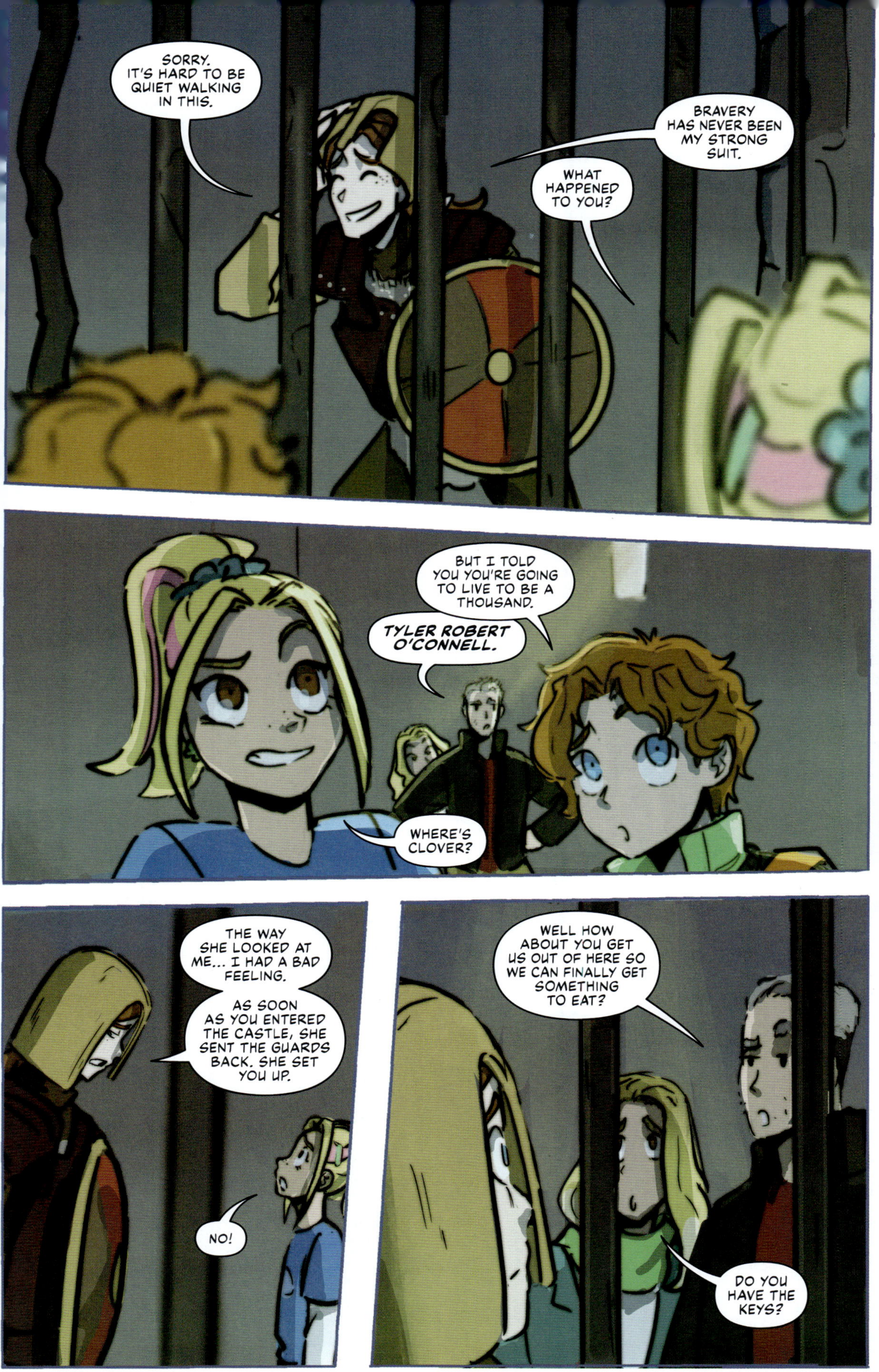

SORRY. IT'S HARD TO BE QUIET WALKING IN THIS.
BRAVERY HAS NEVER BEEN MY STRONG SUIT.
WHAT HAPPENED TO YOU?
BUT I TOLD YOU YOU'RE GOING TO LIVE TO BE A THOUSAND.
TYLER ROBERT O'CONNELL.
WHERE'S CLOVER?
THE WAY SHE LOOKED AT ME... I HAD A BAD FEELING.
AS SOON AS YOU ENTERED THE CASTLE, SHE SENT THE GUARDS BACK. SHE SET YOU UP.
NO!
WELL HOW ABOUT YOU GET US OUT OF HERE SO WE CAN FINALLY GET SOMETHING TO EAT?
DO YOU HAVE THE KEYS?

NO,
BUT...
STAND BACK.
BANG
SEE? I TOLD YOU! THE BARS ARE COMICALLY WEAK!
HURRY!
YOU KNOW, YOU REALLY SHOULD HAVE WARNED US.
"DON'T SHOW YOUR IPHONES AND BRING A JACKET IF YOU TEND TO GET COLD."

CREEEAK
GRRR!
RORY, I PROMISE YOU'LL GET OUT OF THIS FINE!
I'M... GOING TO NEED SOME HELP.
I HAVE AN IDEA.
DAD, YOU'RE A WOLF!
OH, THIS IS MORE FUN THAN I THOUGHT IT'D BE!

READY?
NOT REALLY.
GROAR!
AAAAAAH!
WHAT MAGIC IS THAT?!
EEP!
SLAM
LET'S GO!

MY HERO!
GASP!
GOING SOMEWHERE?
I THINK I FIGURED OUT HOW YOUR POWERS WORK.
STAY BACK!

YOU NEED TO BE TOUCHING A PLANT FOR IT TO GROW.
MOSS?
I KNEW IT!
HEH.
THIS ISN'T STRONG ENOUGH.

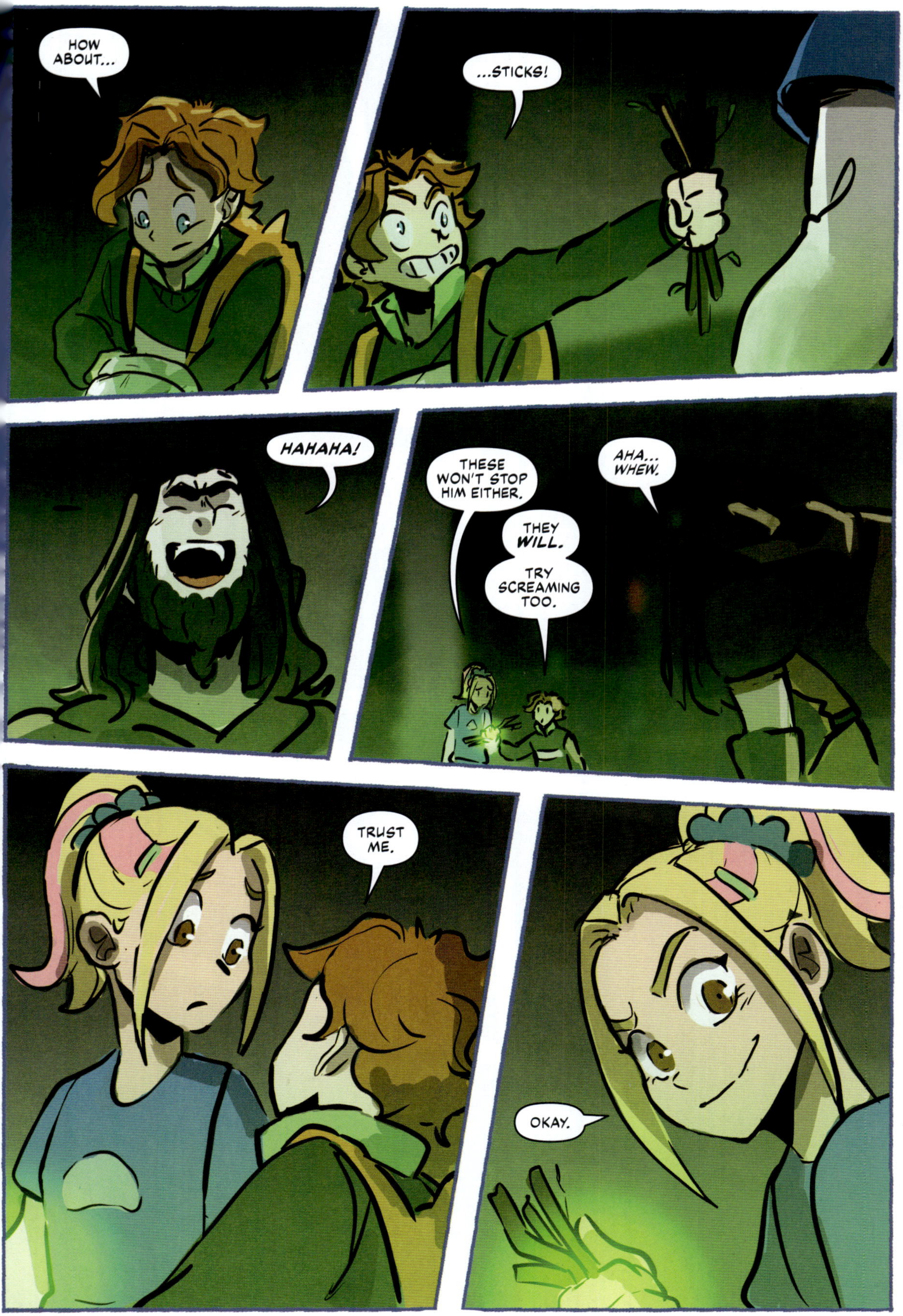
HOW ABOUT...
...STICKS!
HAHAHA!
THESE WON'T STOP HIM EITHER.
AHA... WHEW.
THEY WILL.
TRY SCREAMING TOO.
TRUST ME.
OKAY.

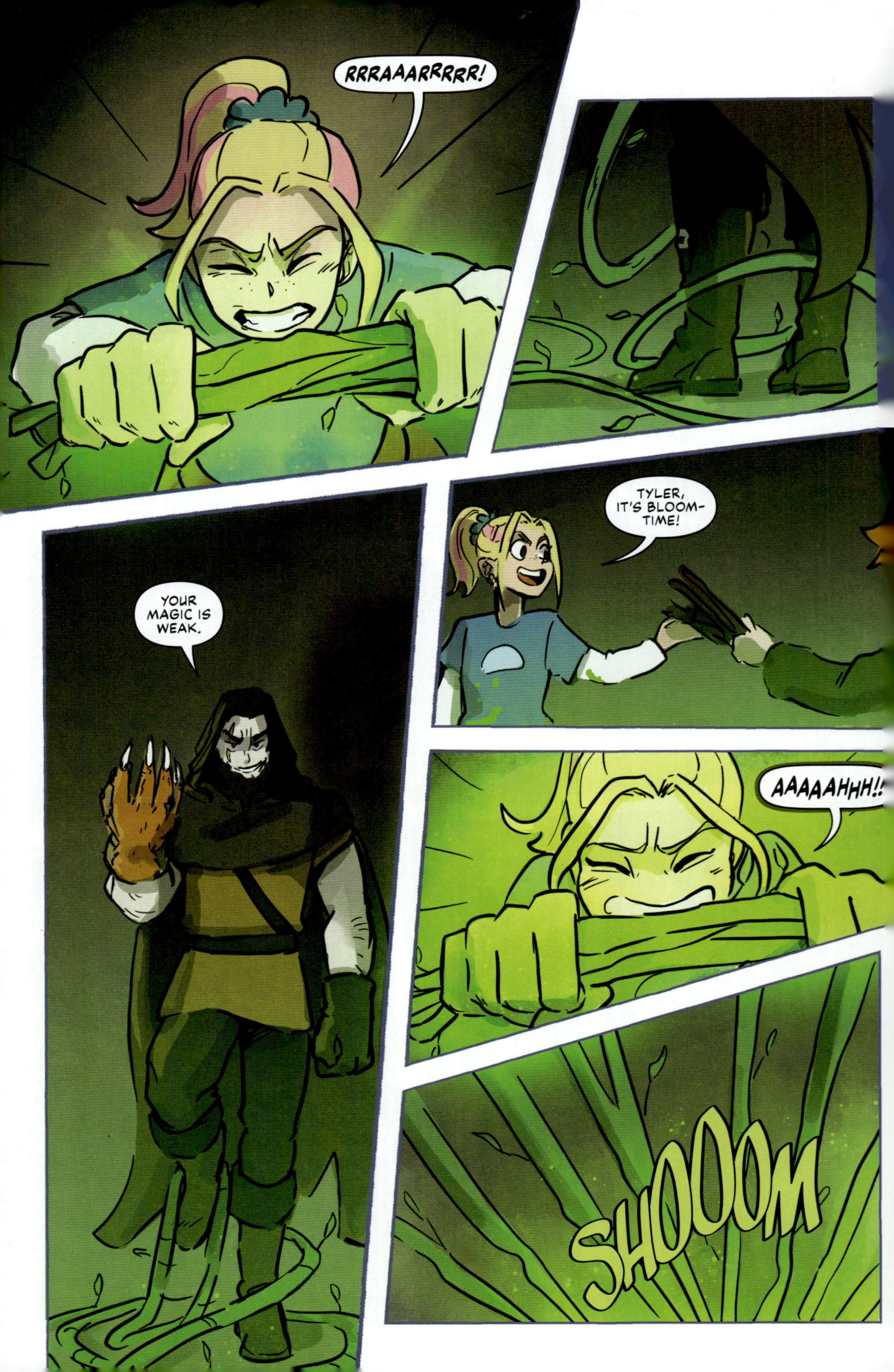
RRRAAARRRRR!
YOUR MAGIC IS WEAK.
TYLER, IT'S BLOOM-TIME!
AAAAAHHH!!
SHOOOM

THWIP
BAM
TAKE THAT, DR. McSCRUFFLE-FINGERS!
WELL DONE.
NOT QUITE.
YOU DID IT!
HI.
IF SHE LIFTS HER HANDS, *KILL* HER PARENTS.

THAT DIALOGUE IS A LITTLE EXTREME FOR THE KIDS, DON'T YOU THINK?
GRR.
GIRL, WHERE ARE YOU?
CUT ME LOOSE.
CLOVER, YOU DOUBLE-CROSSED US?!
OWW.
DROP THE TWIGS.

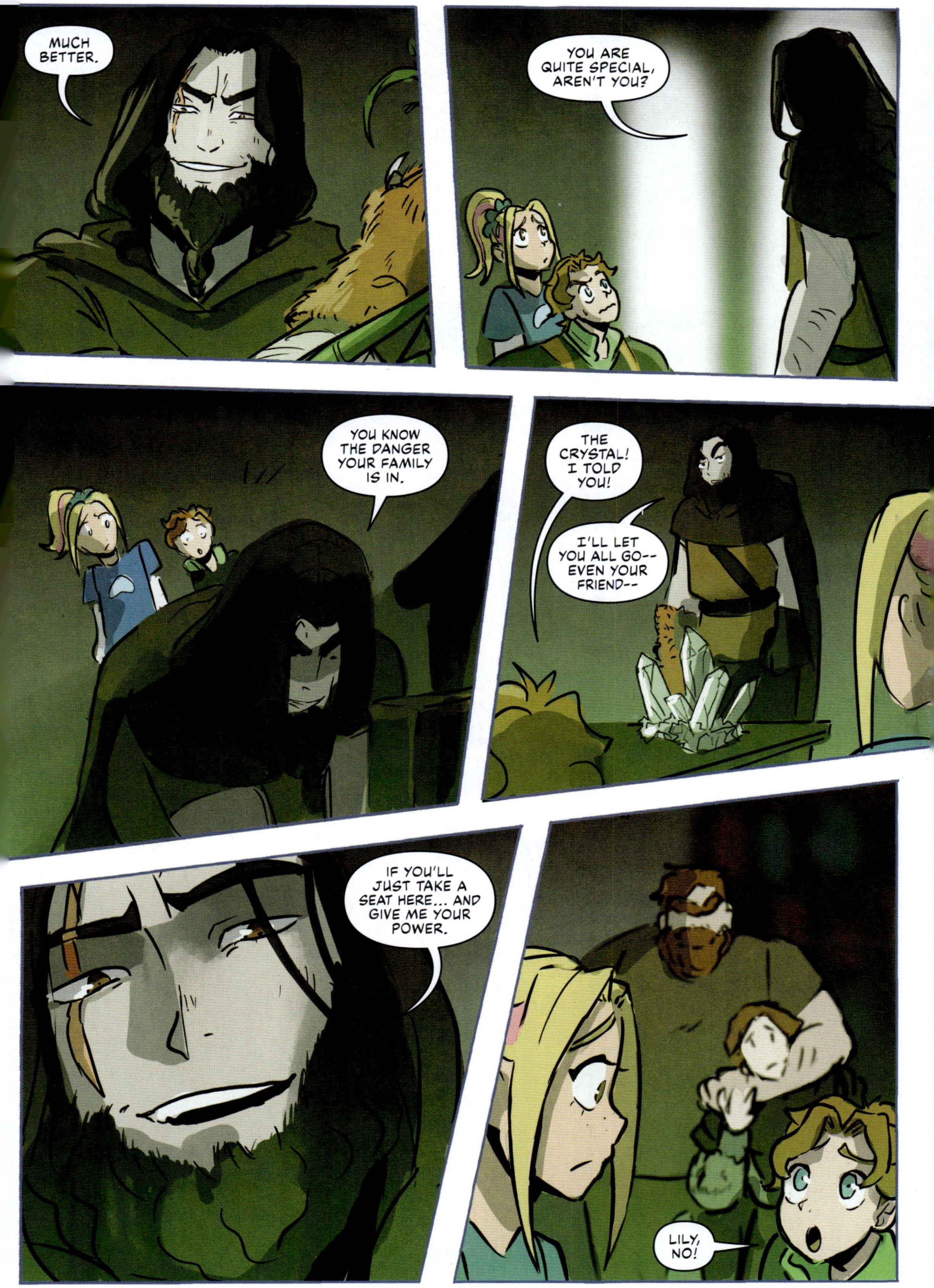

MUCH BETTER.
YOU ARE QUITE SPECIAL, AREN'T YOU?
YOU KNOW THE DANGER YOUR FAMILY IS IN.
THE CRYSTAL! I TOLD YOU!
I'LL LET YOU ALL GO-- EVEN YOUR FRIEND--
IF YOU'LL JUST TAKE A SEAT HERE... AND GIVE ME YOUR POWER.
LILY, NO!

I'LL DO IT.
IF YOU FREE HER TOO.
MY SERVANT?
HER NAME IS CLOVER.
YOU DO KNOW MY GUARDS RECAPTURED YOU AND YOUR BROTHER BECAUSE OF HER.
I DO.
SO WE HAVE A DEAL?
WHY NOT?

OF THE MANY WONDERS I HAVE LEARNED ABOUT--BEFORE TODAY--THE MOST FANTASTIC IS A CRYSTAL THAT CAN HARNESS THE POWER OF OTHERS.
I SEARCHED FOR YEARS, ALWAYS KNOWING I WOULD EVENTUALLY FIND IT.
IT IS MY DESTINY TO RULE.
SO PREDICTABLE. THIS IS WHEN THE BAD GUYS ALWAYS TAKE TOO LONG EXPLAINING THEIR PLANS, WHICH ALLOWS THE GOOD GUYS TO WIN.
NOW THAT I POSSESS THIS CRYSTAL--FORGED IN THE EYES OF THE GODS AND COVETED BY KINGS SINCE THE DAWN OF TIME--
HE'S LAYING IT ON A BIT THICK!
--NOTHING CAN STOP ME. THE CRYSTAL ALREADY HOLDS POWER WE CANNOT IMAGINE.
AND NOW WE ADD YOURS.

AS SOON AS I--
IS THIS WHERE HE GETS HIS COMEUPPANCE?
I JUST GOT IT TODAY.
WAIT A MINUTE.
MAYBE IF WE BOTH...
AHA!
NEAT TRICK.
IT'S DONE! THE POWER IS MINE!
WHAT WAS IT... WRITTEN UNDER THE PAINTING?
CLOVER, IN THE FUTURE, RORY HAS YOUR PORTRAIT HANGING ABOVE HIS FIREPLACE. YOU'RE THE LOVE OF HIS LIFE.
LOOK, I KNOW THIS ISN'T MAKING SENSE NOW, BUT I SWEAR TO YOU IT WILL.
IF I'VE LEARNED ANYTHING TODAY, IT'S THAT...

"ONE DAY CAN CHANGE EVERYTHING."
RORY SAID YOUR FATHER USED TO TELL YOU THAT.
BUT I'VE NEVER TOLD ANYONE.
NOW THAT I HAVE YOUR POWERS... AND IT'S CLEAR TO ME YOU'RE ALL JUST REGULAR HUMANS AND NOT FAIRIES...
TAKE THEM TO THE GRAVEYARD.
OOOH... SCARY!
HE SAID HE'D LET US GO, BUT HE DIDN'T SAY HIS HENCHMEN WOULD. CLASSIC!

NO!
PUT IT DOWN.
OR YOU DIE TOO.
CIARAN, MAY THE CAT EAT YOU...
CLOVER, LOOK OUT!
WHAM

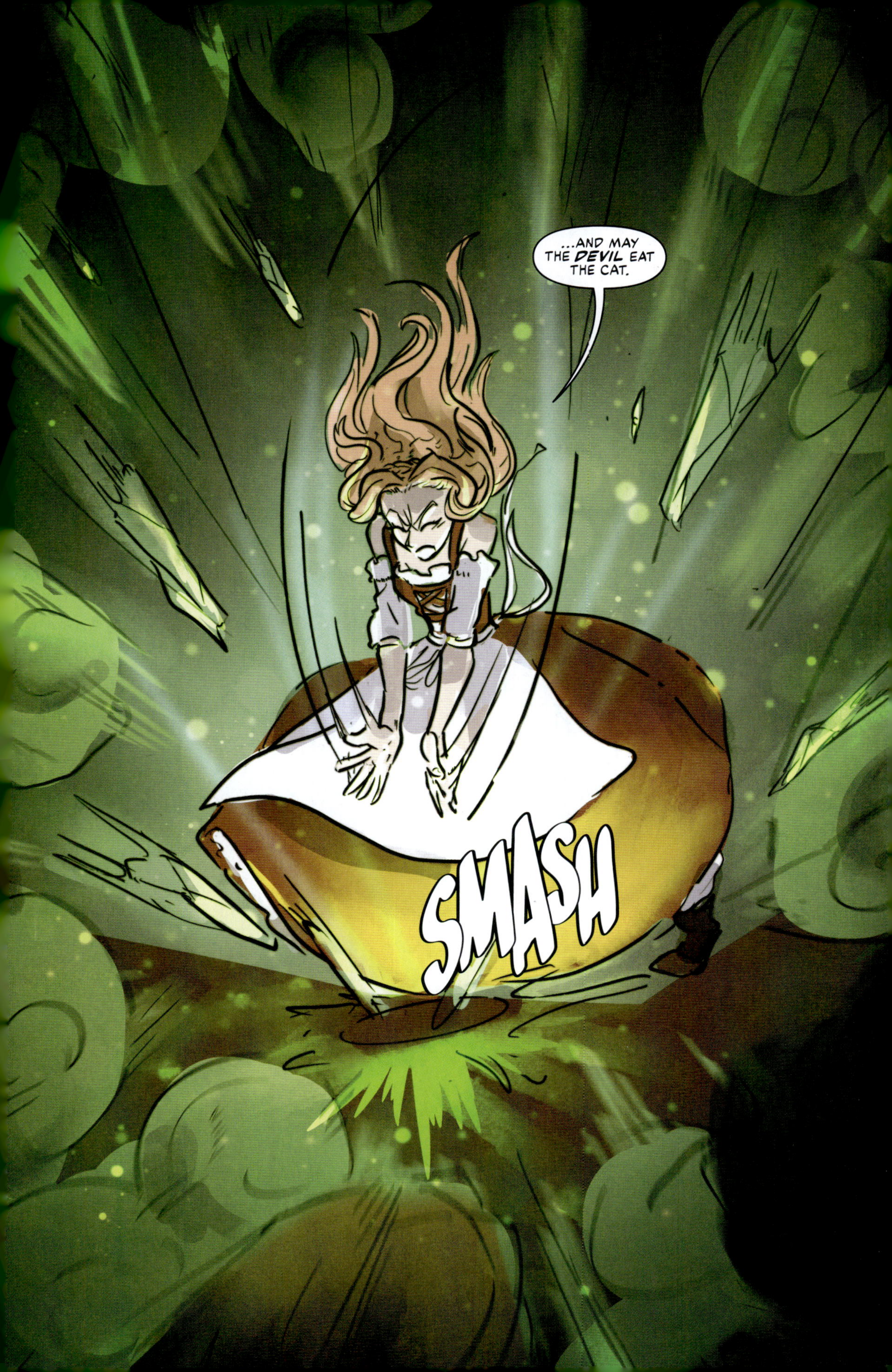
...AND MAY THE DEVIL EAT THE CAT.
SMASH

KOFF
RUN!
WOW! BRAVO!
CLAP CLAP CLAP
GOOD SHOW! I REALLY STAN YOU GUYS.
OOPS.

DON'T WANT TO FORGET MY PHONE.
GREAT DISAPPEARING ACT BY THE WAY.
DARN... OUT OF BATTERY.
ALMOST BELIEVABLE!
THAT'S YOUR WORST NIGHTMARE!
IRL.
THAT'S "IN REAL LIFE" IN AMERICAN TEENAGE SLANG...
...WHICH I NOW UNDERSTAND I SHOULD STOP USING.
OKAY, THEN... BACK TO THE HOTEL?
THAT WAS FUN!

WHERE'S CIARAN?
MAYBE HIS POWER WAS TIED TO THE CRYSTAL, AND WHEN IT BROKE...
BYE BYE, DR. MCSCRUFFLE-FINGERS.
HEH.
HAHAHAHAHAHAHAHA!
DID YOU SEE THE GREEN SMOKE?
I THINK I GOT IT IN MY MOUTH.

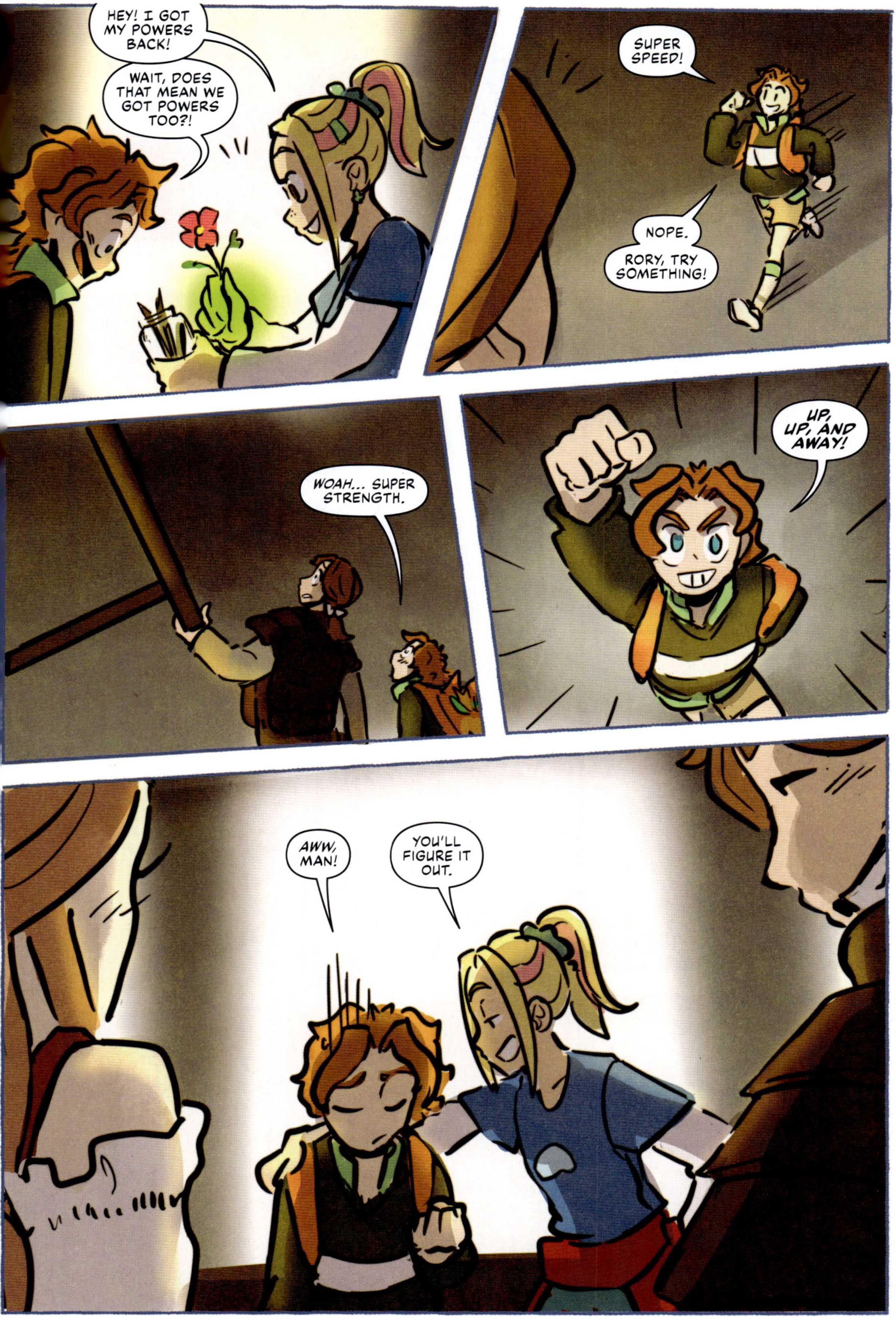
HEY! I GOT MY POWERS BACK!
WAIT, DOES THAT MEAN WE GOT POWERS TOO?!
SUPER SPEED!
NOPE.
RORY, TRY SOMETHING!
WOAH... SUPER STRENGTH.
UP, UP, AND AWAY!
AWW, MAN!
YOU'LL FIGURE IT OUT.

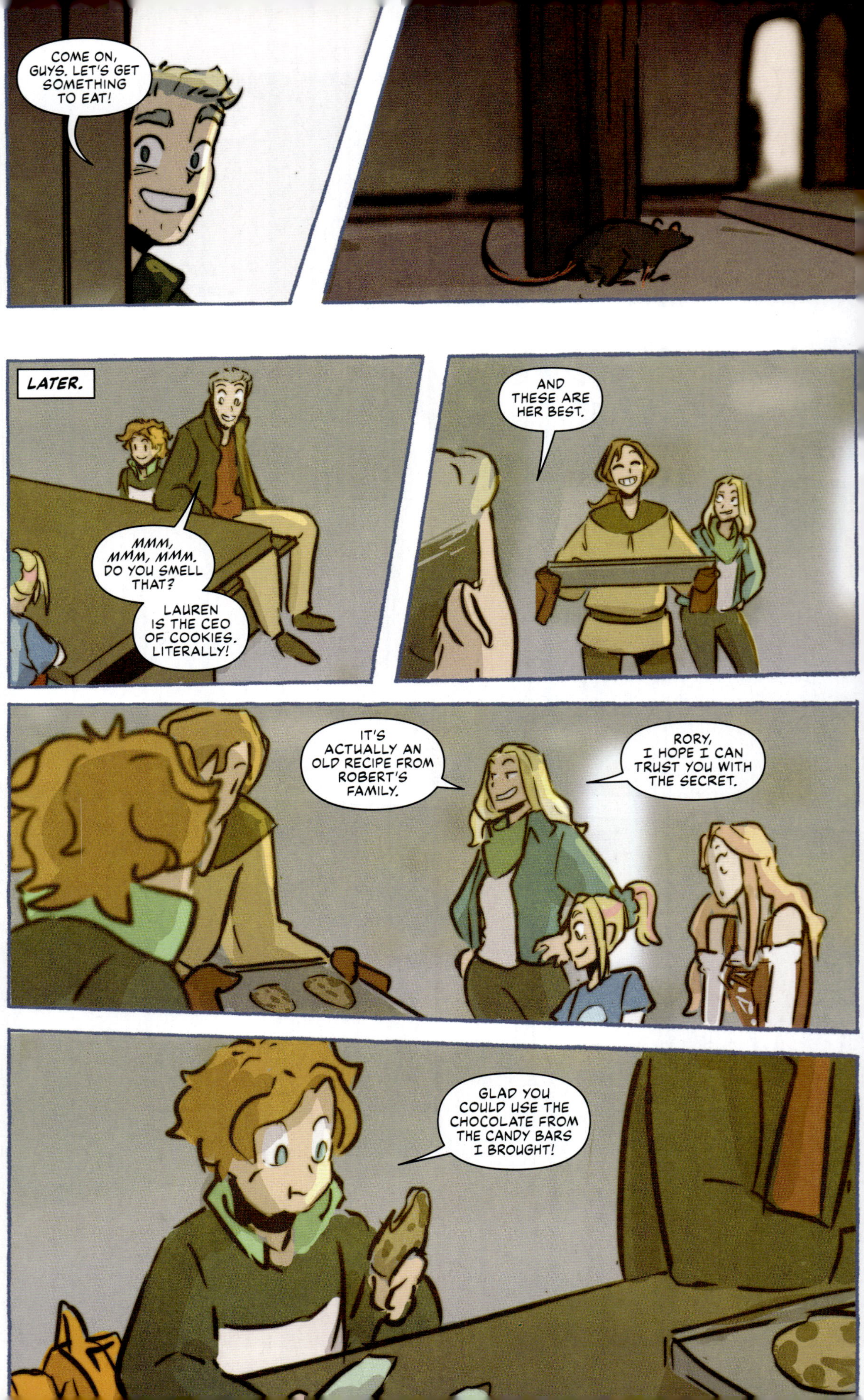
COME ON, GUYS, LET'S GET SOMETHING TO EAT!
LATER.
MMM, MMM, MMM. DO YOU SMELL THAT?
LAUREN IS THE CEO OF COOKIES. LITERALLY!
AND THESE ARE HER BEST.
IT'S ACTUALLY AN OLD RECIPE FROM ROBERT'S FAMILY.
RORY, I HOPE I CAN TRUST YOU WITH THE SECRET.
GLAD YOU COULD USE THE CHOCOLATE FROM THE CANDY BARS I BROUGHT!

NOW LET'S SEE IF THE PUZZLE MASTER CAN PUT THE BROKEN CRYSTAL BACK TOGETHER AGAIN.
DAD AND I WILL CLEAN UP.
YOU'RE SURE THIS WILL WORK?
TYLER SAYS IT WILL. AND I BELIEVE HIM.
ADDING THIS LAST PIECE WILL SEND US HOME.
THEN I TAKE THE CRYSTAL APART AND KEEP THE PIECES SAFE?
FOR THE NEXT THOUSAND YEARS, UNTIL WE MEET YOU--THE OLD YOU--ON OUR FAMILY VACATION TO IRELAND.
IT HURTS MY HEAD JUST THINKING ABOUT IT.
IT DOES MAKE AS MUCH SENSE AS MANY OF THE THINGS THAT HAPPENED TODAY.
ALL FINISHED. TIME TO HIT THE HAY, KIDS. THE TIME ZONE CHANGE CAUGHT UP WITH ME ALL OF A SUDDEN.
OR MAYBE YOU JUST ATE EIGHT OF MOM'S COOKIES!
YOU REMEMBER EVERYTHING I TOLD YOU?
I KNOW WHEN TO BE WHERE.
WHAT WILL YOU DO NOW?

WELL, SINCE YOU TOLD ME I'LL BE FINE NO MATTER WHAT CRAZY THINGS I DO...
...THERE ARE A COUPLE OF THINGS I'M GOING TO MUSTER UP THE COURAGE TO TRY.
YOU KNOW ANOTHER THING PEOPLE SAY ABOUT THESE SPECIAL CLOVERS?
THEY ARE HARD TO FIND AND VERY LUCKY TO HAVE.
JUST LIKE TRUE LOVE.
YOU SHOULD HOLD ONTO IT THEN.
I THINK IT'S TIME.

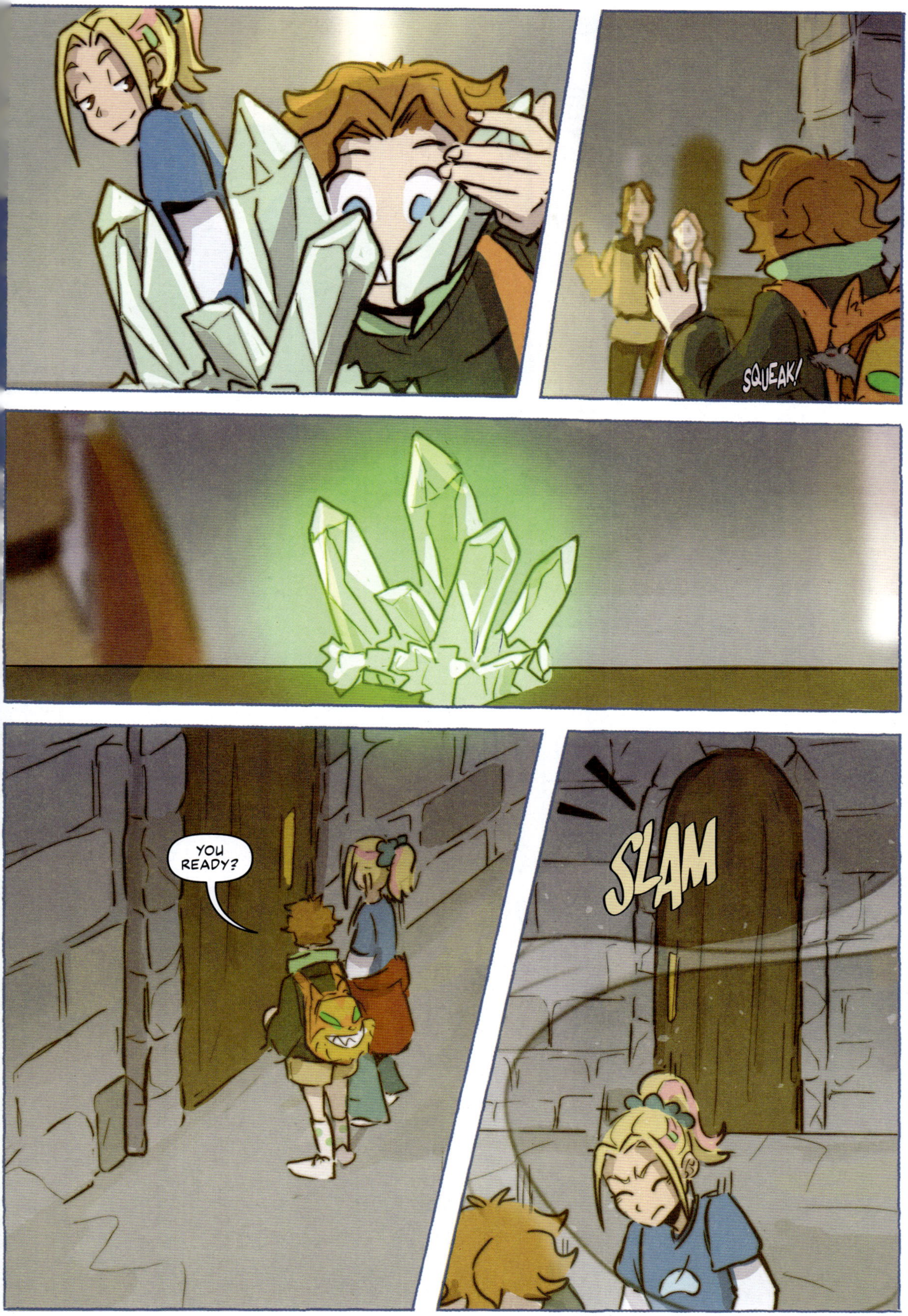
SQUEAK!
YOU READY?
SLAM

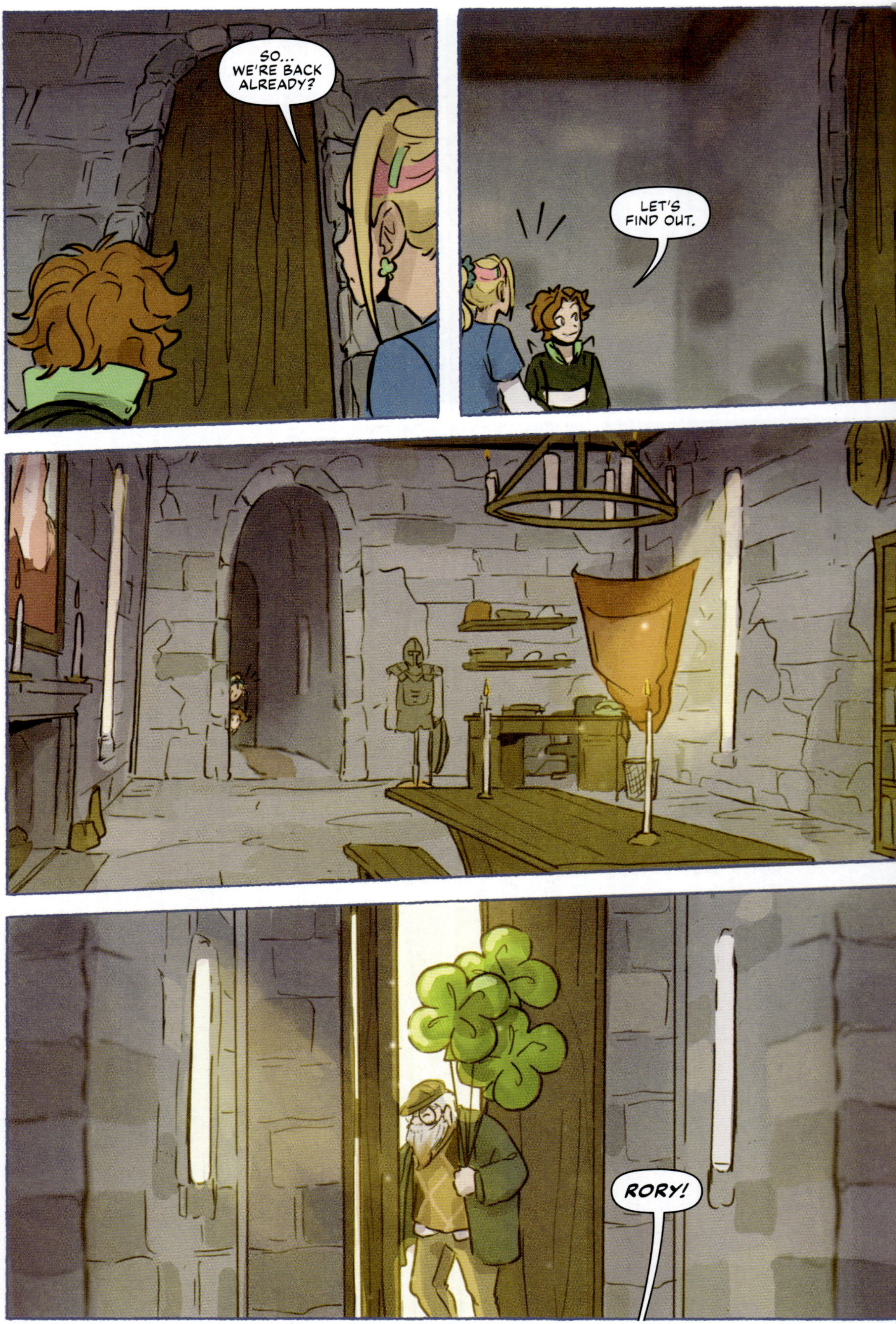
SO... WE'RE BACK ALREADY?
LET'S FIND OUT.
RORY!

AH, KIDS. IT WAS SO TOUGH NOT TO HUG YOU AT THE AIRPORT.
SO IT REALLY IS YOU? RORY FROM ANCIENT IRELAND?
TOLD YOU!
IT HAS BEEN... A LONG TIME. I HAVE SO MUCH TO SHARE.
BUT THIS IS WHAT I'VE REALLY BEEN WAITING TO SHOW YOU!
THIS IS YOUR FAMILY TREE...
THERE'S YOU, RORY CONALL.

AND CLOVER!
YOU HAD TWO CHILDREN?!
WE DID.
BUT THAT'S A STORY FOR ANOTHER TIME.
WHAT I WANT TO SHOW YOU NOW...
US?!
O'CONNELL MEANS--
DESCENDED FROM WOLVES!
THE SPELLING GOT CHANGED A BIT OVER TIME, BUT--
WAIT, THAT MEANS YOU'RE OUR...

YOUR 40TH GREAT GRANDFATHER. IS IT A LOT TO PROCESS?
HEY!
CLOVER!
YOU HAVE SLOW-AGING POWERS TOO?!
NO, DEAR.
MY LOVE.
I THOUGHT I'D LOST YOU FOREVER THIS TIME.

I'M SO SORRY. CIARAN--
DR. McSCRUFFLE-FINGERS?!
HE IMPRISONED ME.
WHERE?
THE BETTER QUESTION IS ***WHEN.***
MORE TIME TRAVEL?!
LOTS MORE.
FOR ALL OF US.
WE'RE GETTING AHEAD OF OURSELVES, AREN'T WE?
LILY AND TYLER, YOU AND YOUR PARENTS ARE GOING TO HAVE A LOVELY VACATION IN IRELAND.
PRESENT DAY IRELAND, THAT IS.
AND THEN IT'S TIME FOR US TO ***SAVE THE WORLD!***

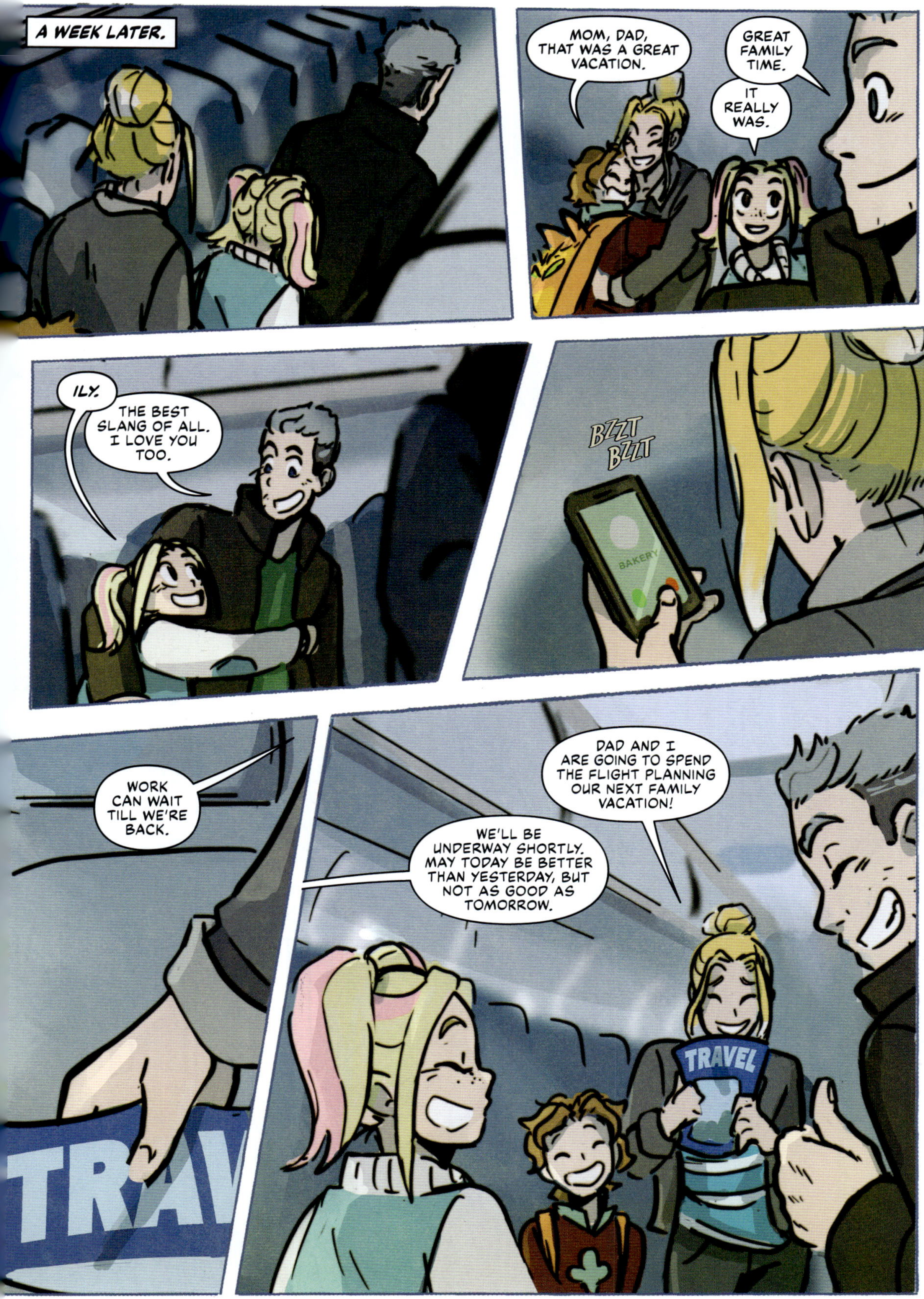
A WEEK LATER.
MOM, DAD, THAT WAS A GREAT VACATION.
GREAT FAMILY TIME.
IT REALLY WAS.
ILY.
THE BEST SLANG OF ALL. I LOVE YOU TOO.
BZZT BZZT
BAKERY
WORK CAN WAIT TILL WE'RE BACK.
TRAV
DAD AND I ARE GOING TO SPEND THE FLIGHT PLANNING OUR NEXT FAMILY VACATION!
WE'LL BE UNDERWAY SHORTLY. MAY TODAY BE BETTER THAN YESTERDAY, BUT NOT AS GOOD AS TOMORROW.
TRAVEL

OOOF! SERIOUSLY, TYLER, DID LEPRECHAUNS FILL YOUR SUITCASE WITH GOLD?
I ALREADY ADMITTED I WAS...
WHAAAAT?!
ACTUALLY, MAYBE THEY DID!

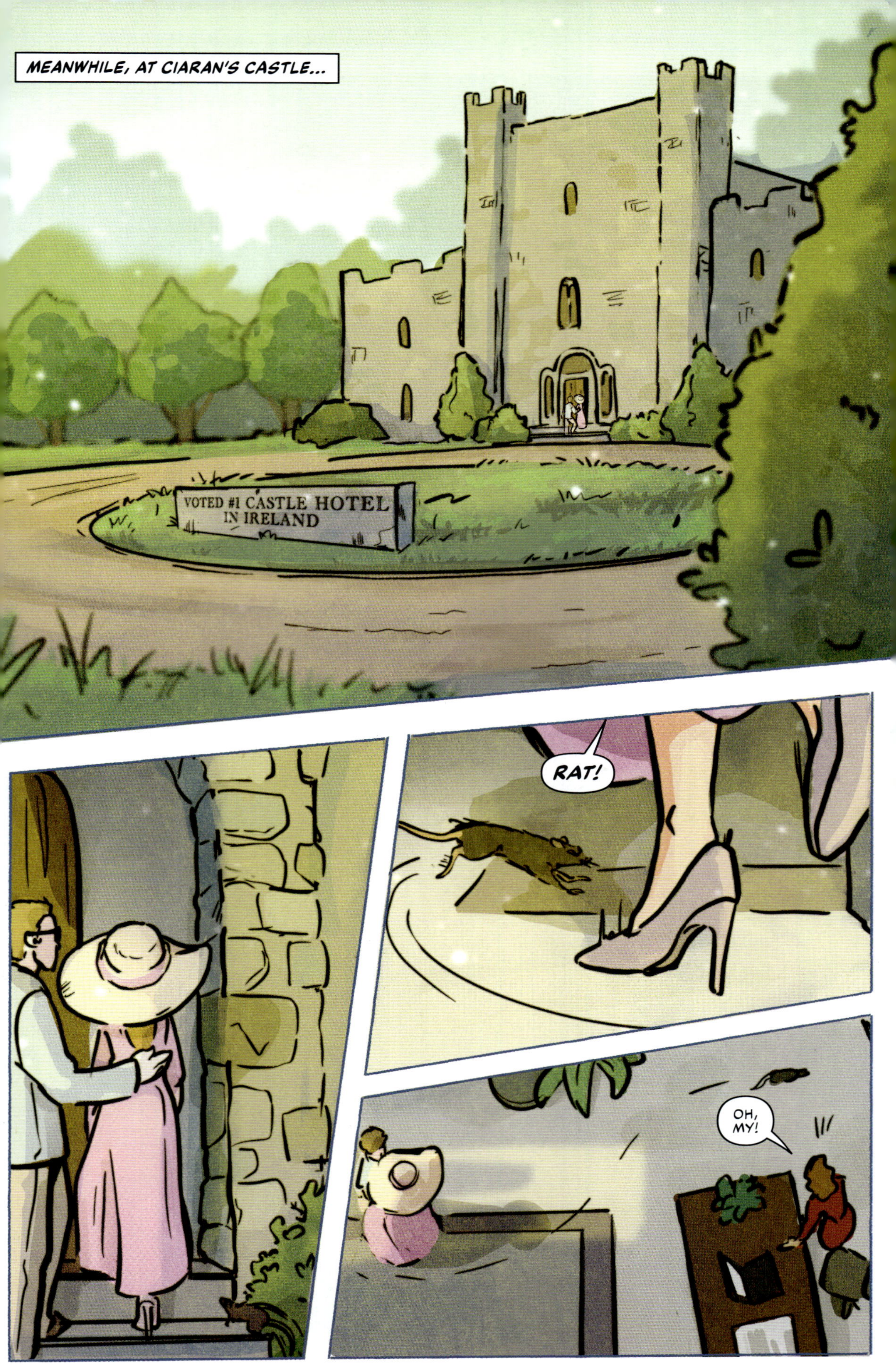
MEANWHILE, AT CIARAN'S CASTLE...
VOTED #1 CASTLE HOTEL IN IRELAND
RAT!
OH, MY!

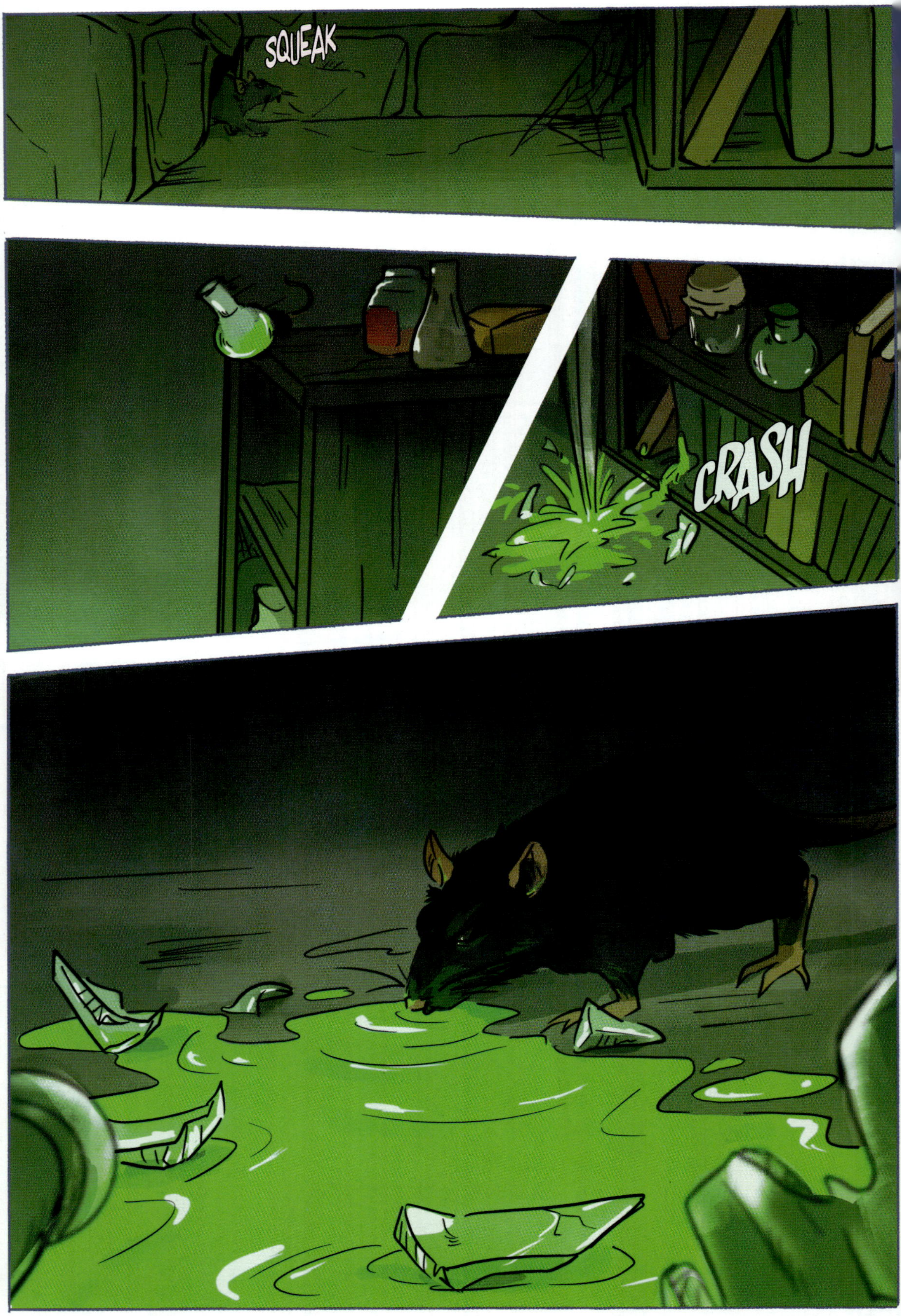
SQUEAK
CRASH

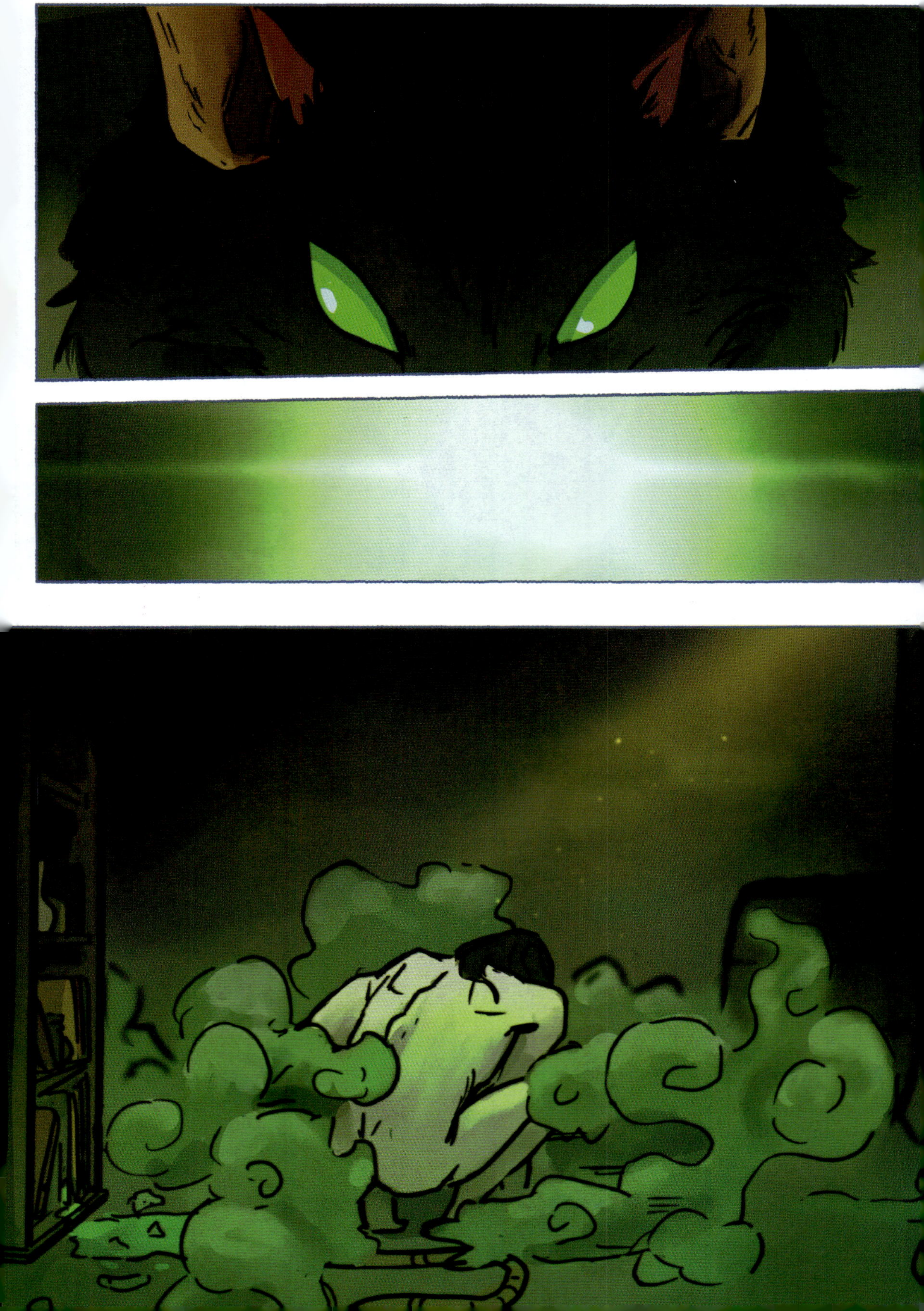

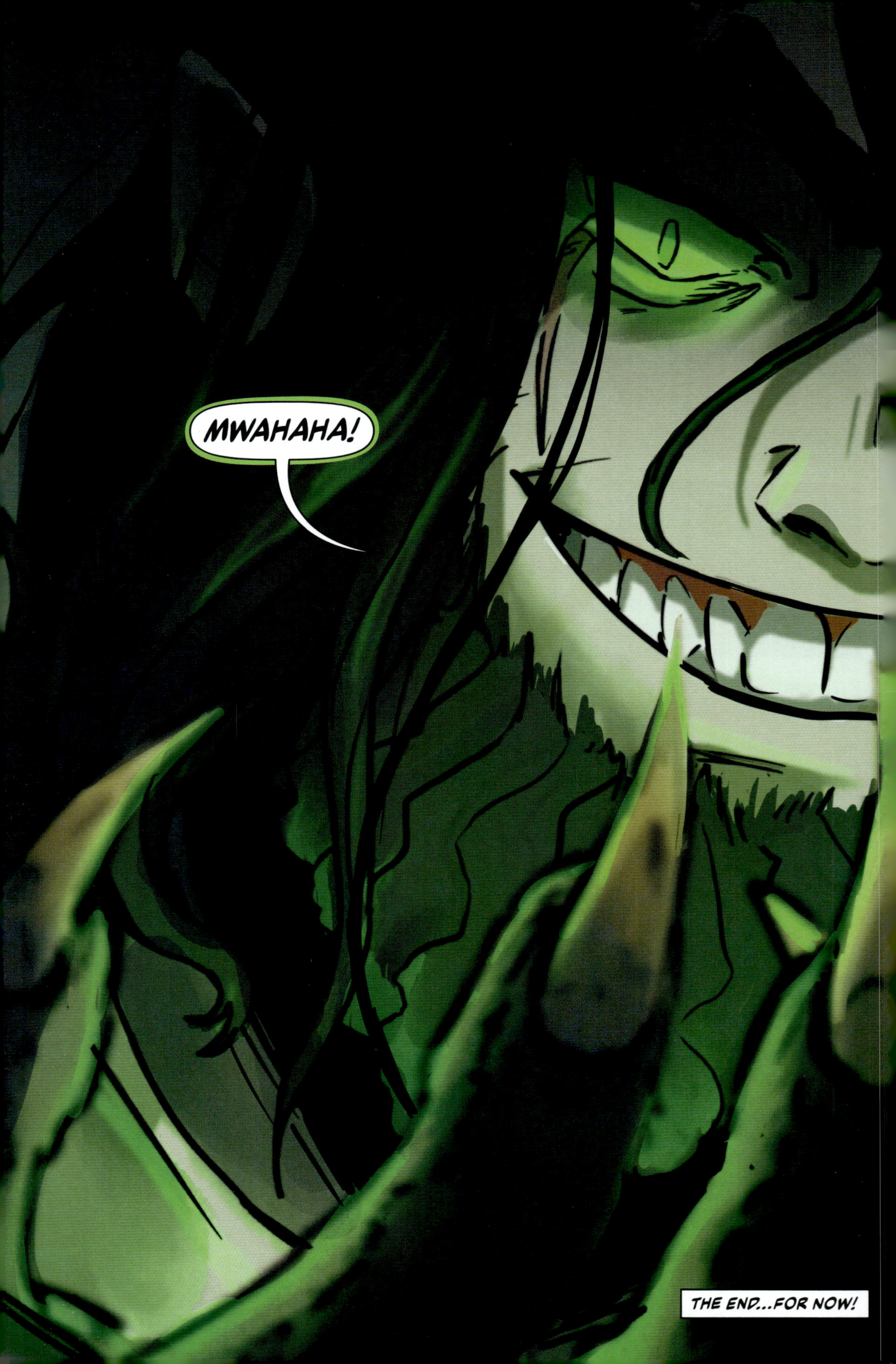
MWAHAHA!
THE END...FOR NOW!

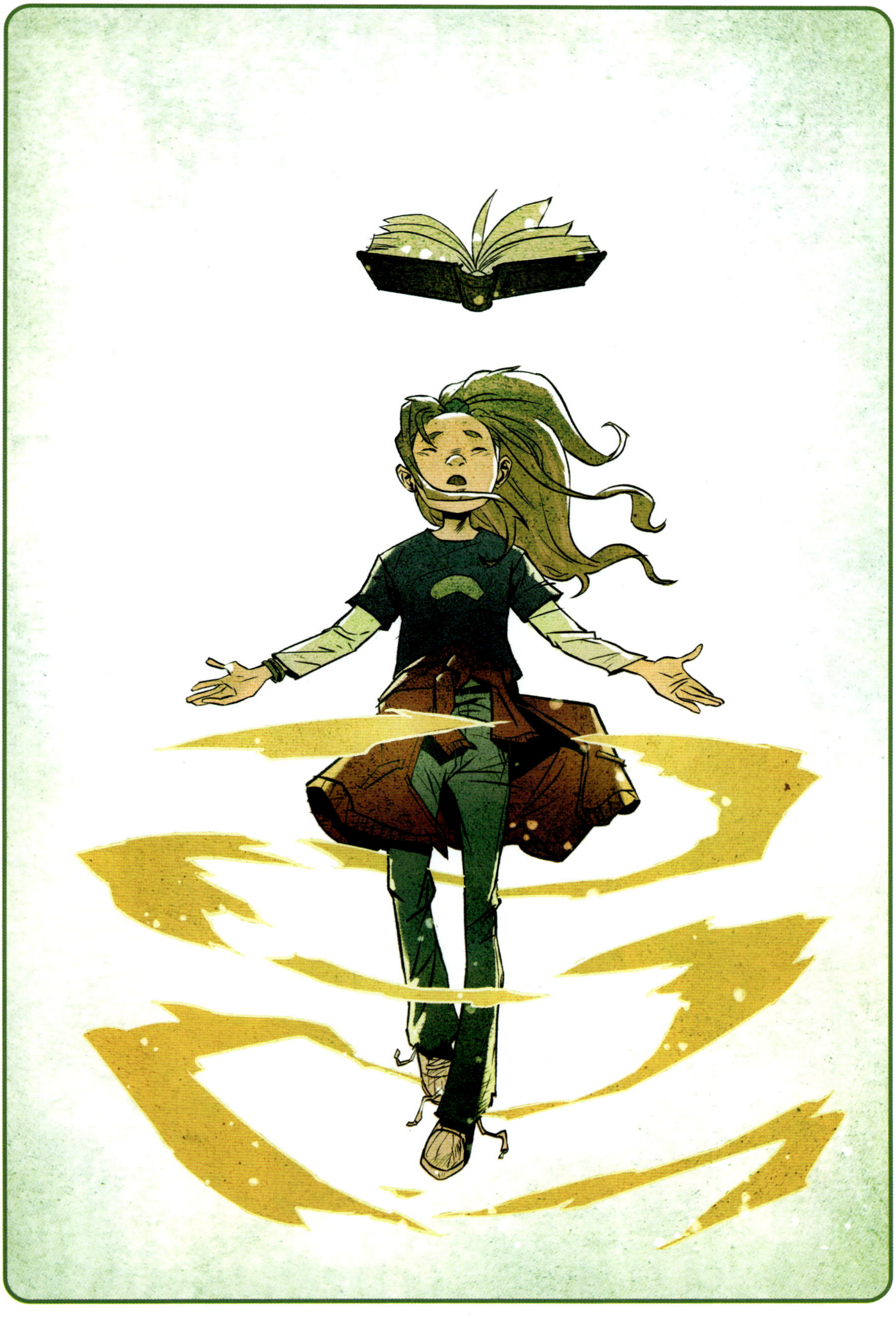

#1 VARIANT COVER
BY **SANFORD GREENE**

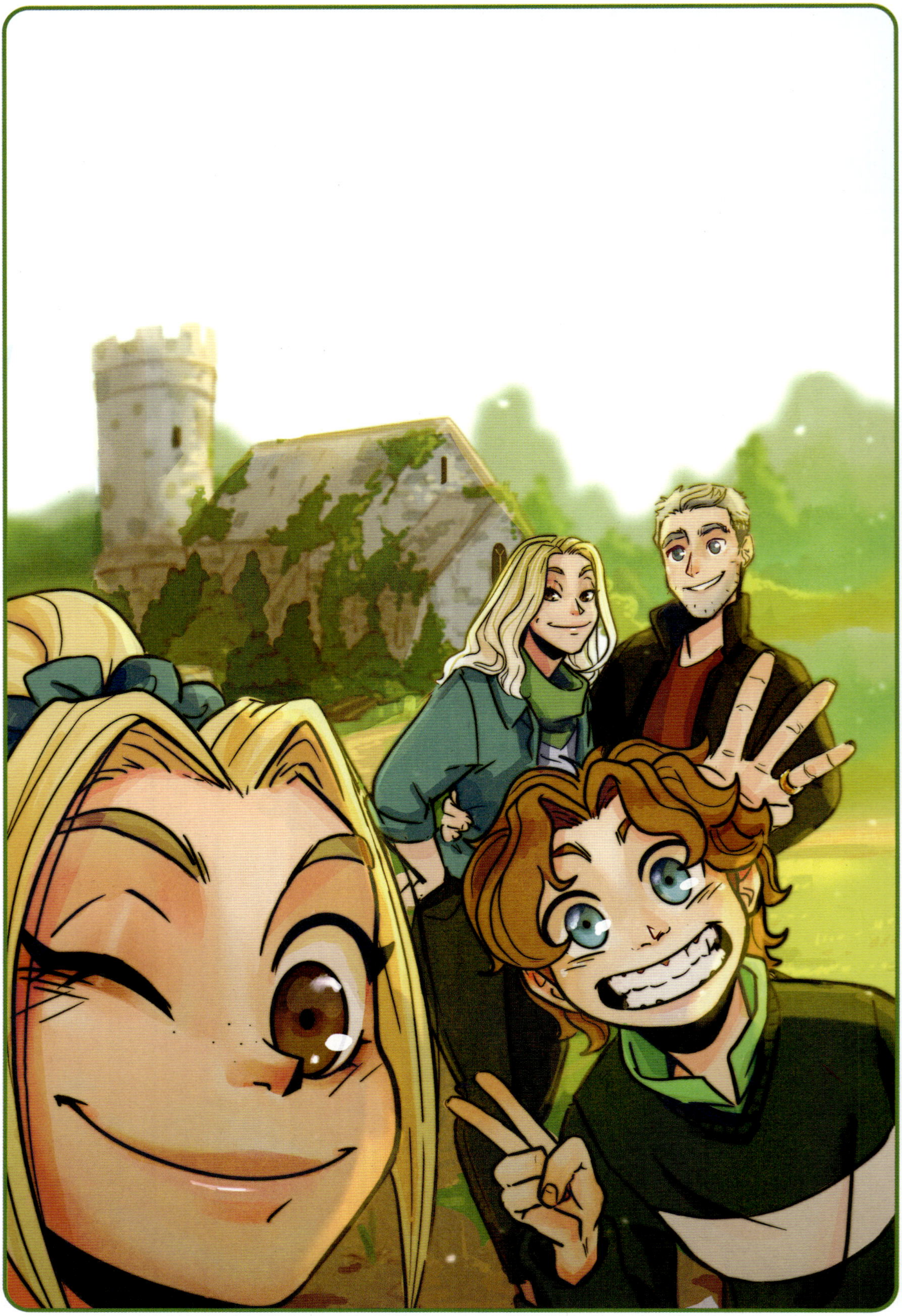

#1 VARIANT COVER
BY **ASIAH FULMORE**

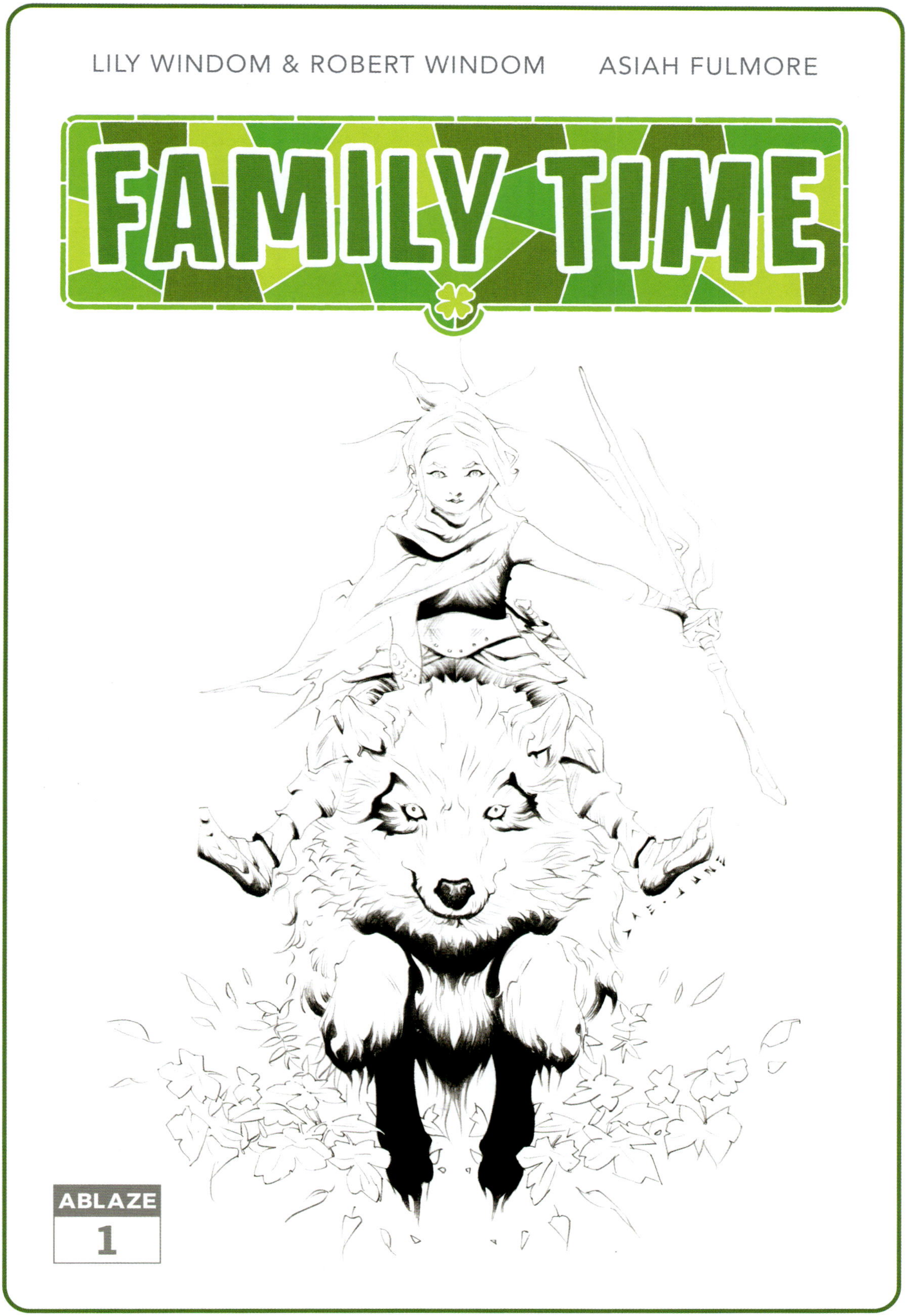
LILY WINDOM & ROBERT WINDOM
ASIAH FULMORE
FAMILY TIME
ABLAZE
1

#1 VARIANT COVER
BY **JAE LEE**

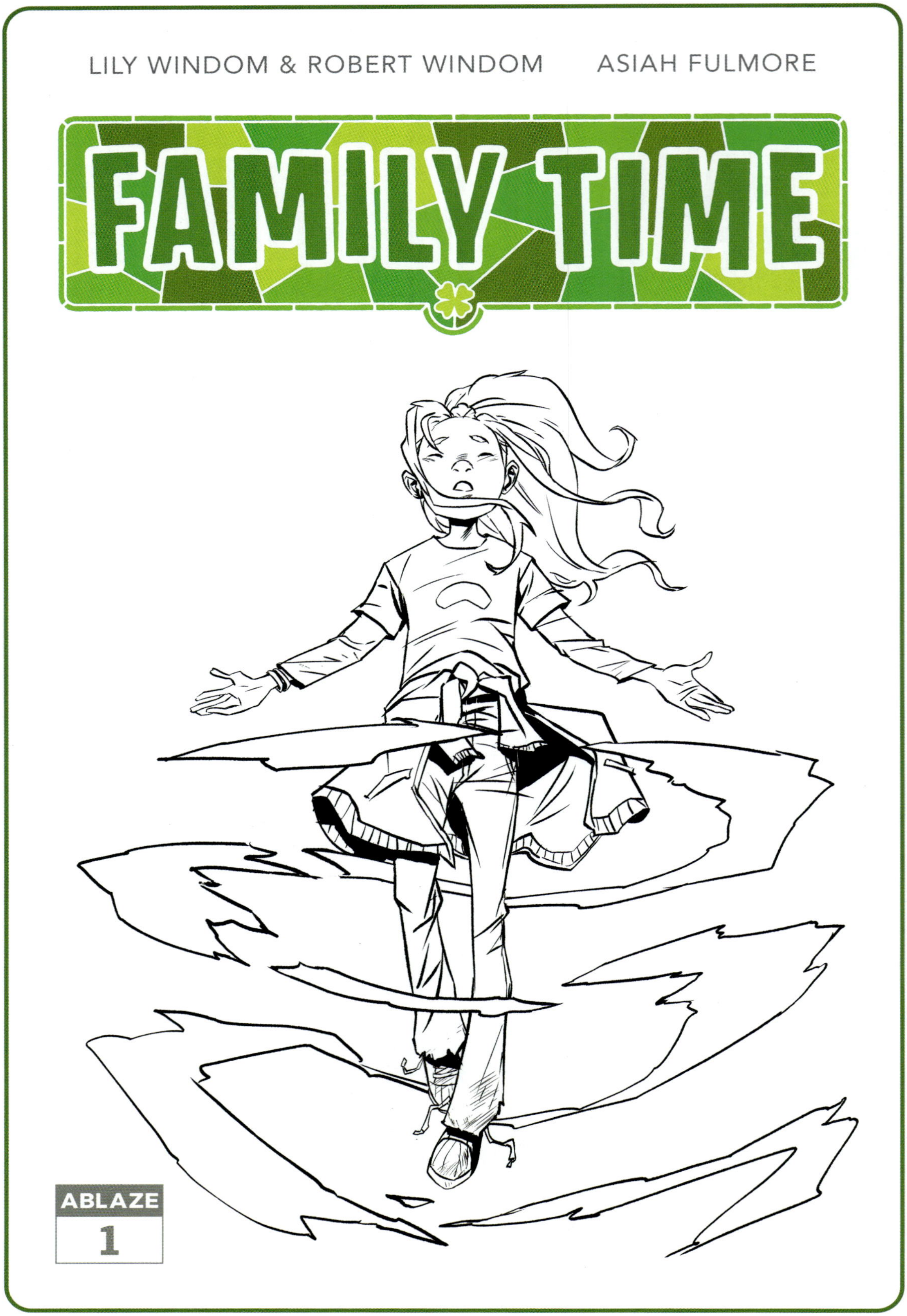

LILY WINDOM & ROBERT WINDOM
ASIAH FULMORE
FAMILY TIME
ABLAZE
1

#1 VARIANT COVER
BY **SANFORD GREENE**

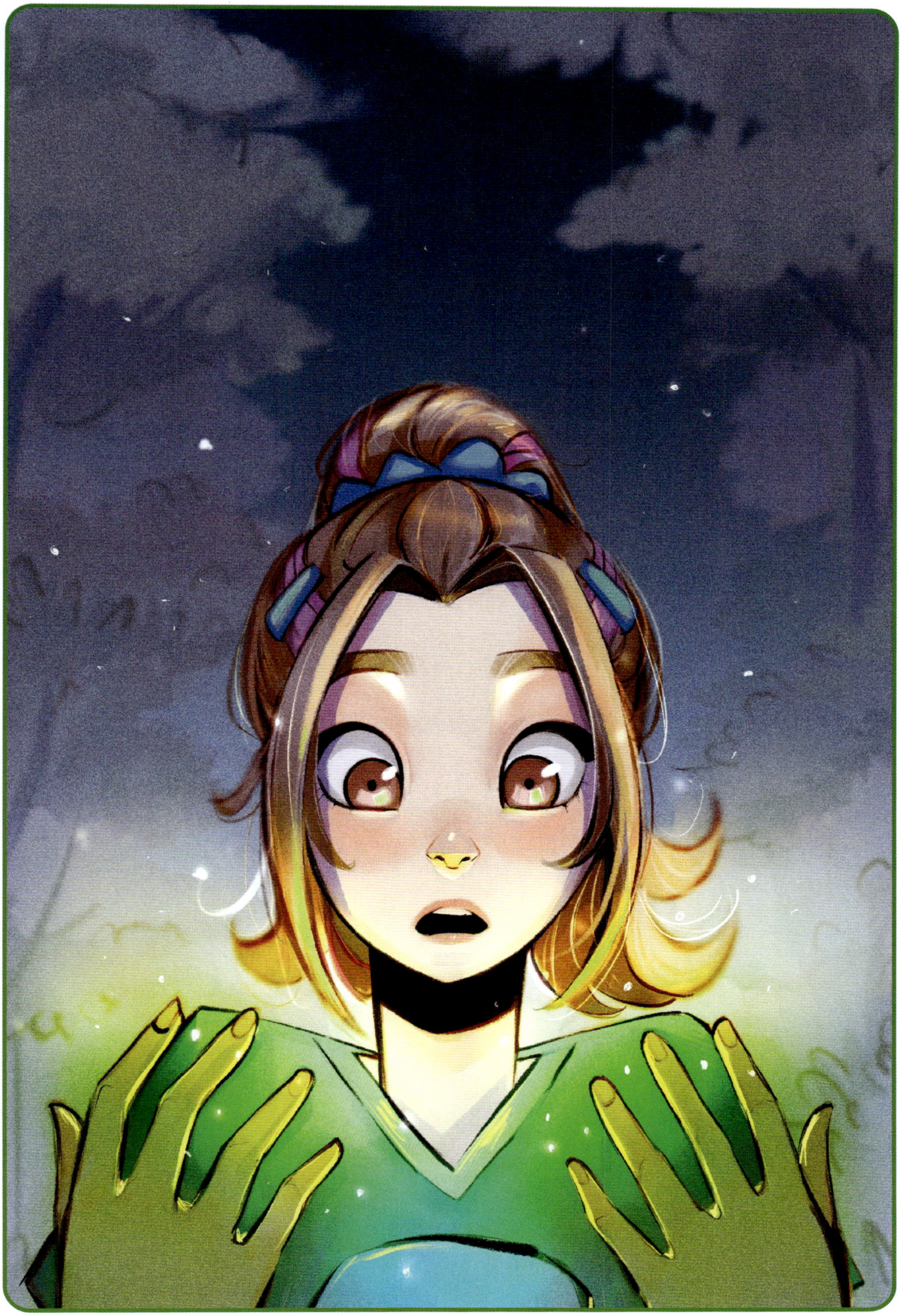

#2 VARIANT COVER
BY **MUZENIK**

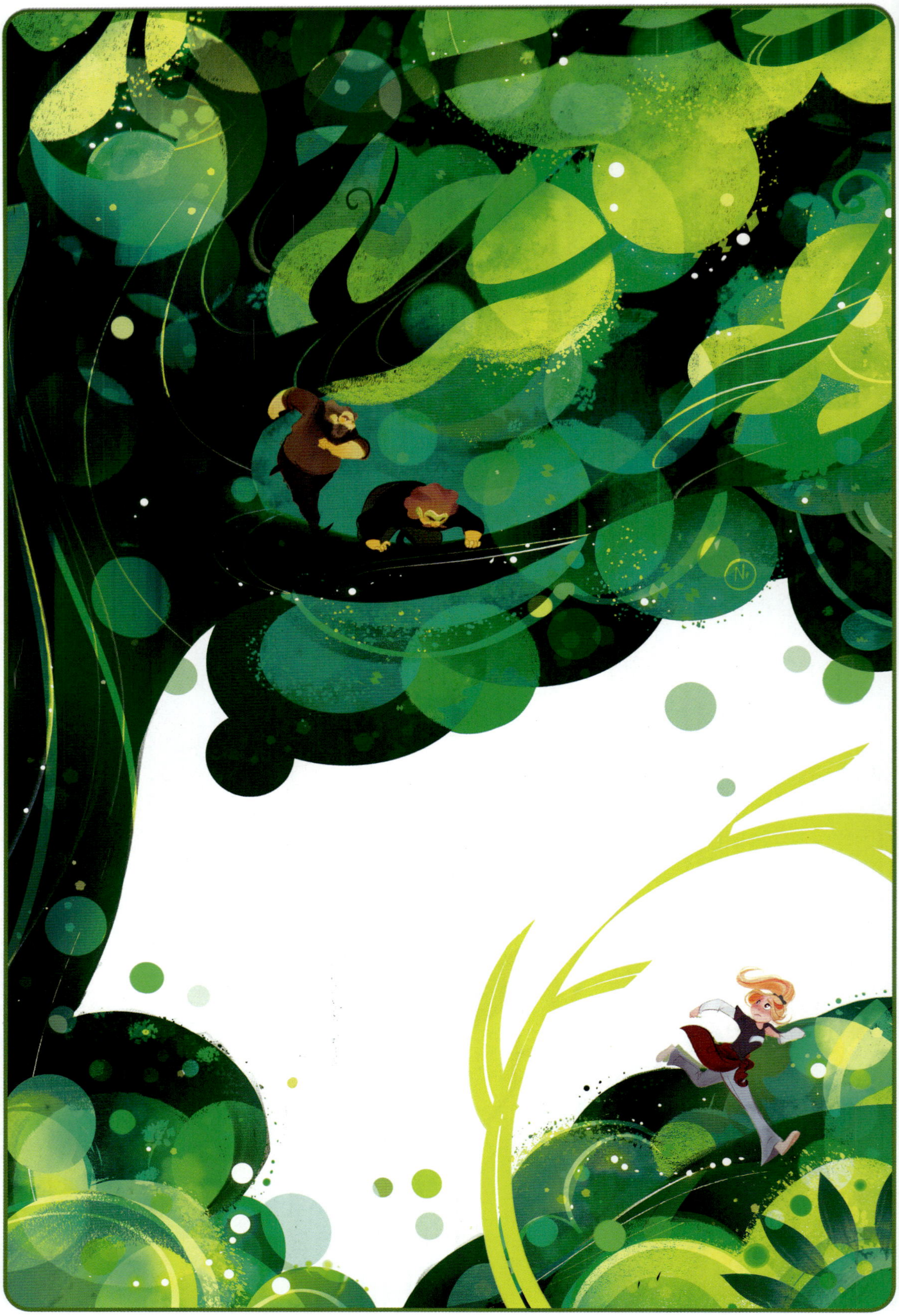

#2 VARIANT COVER
BY **NICOLETTA BALDARI**

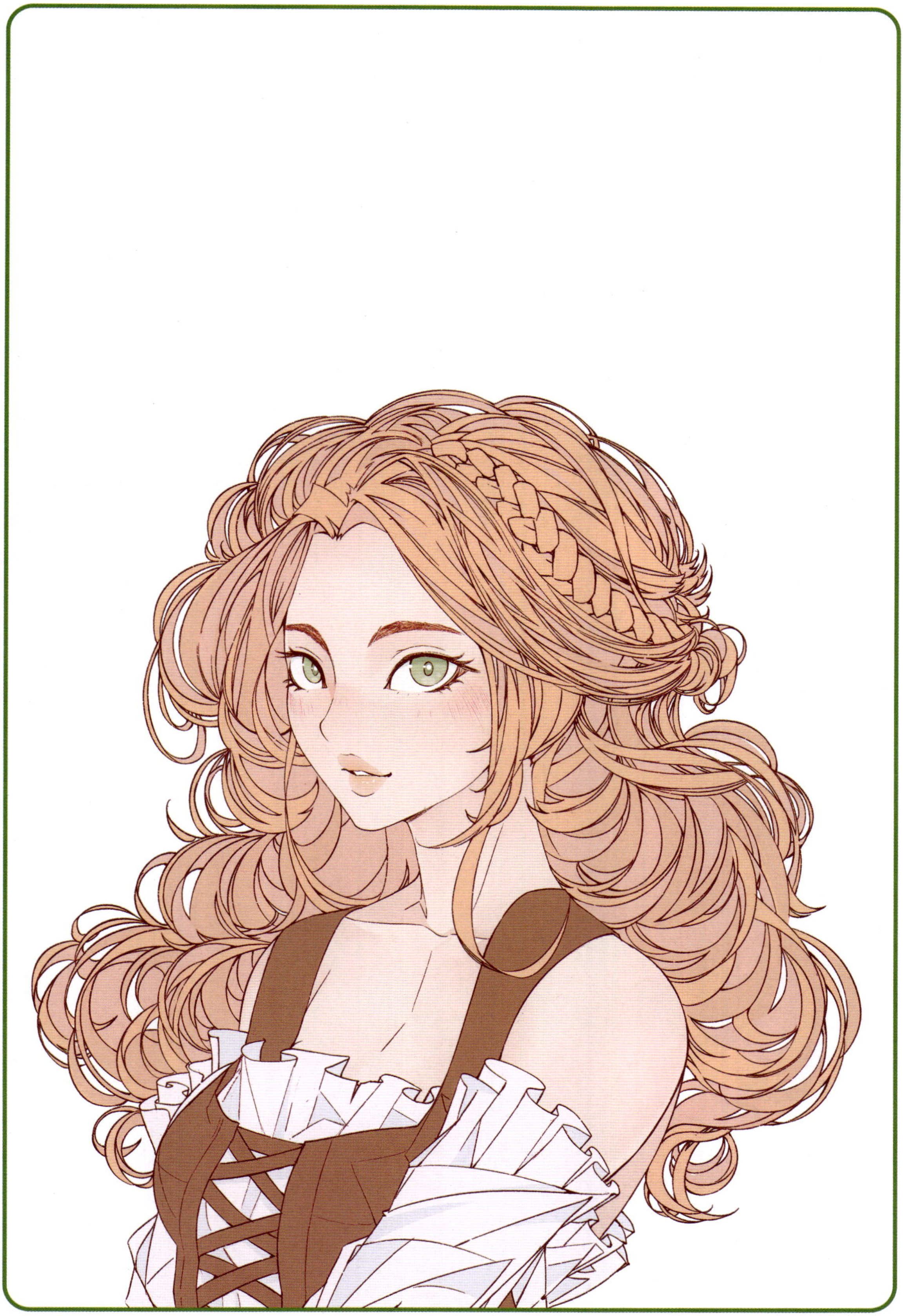

#3 VARIANT COVER
BY **ERI CRUZ**

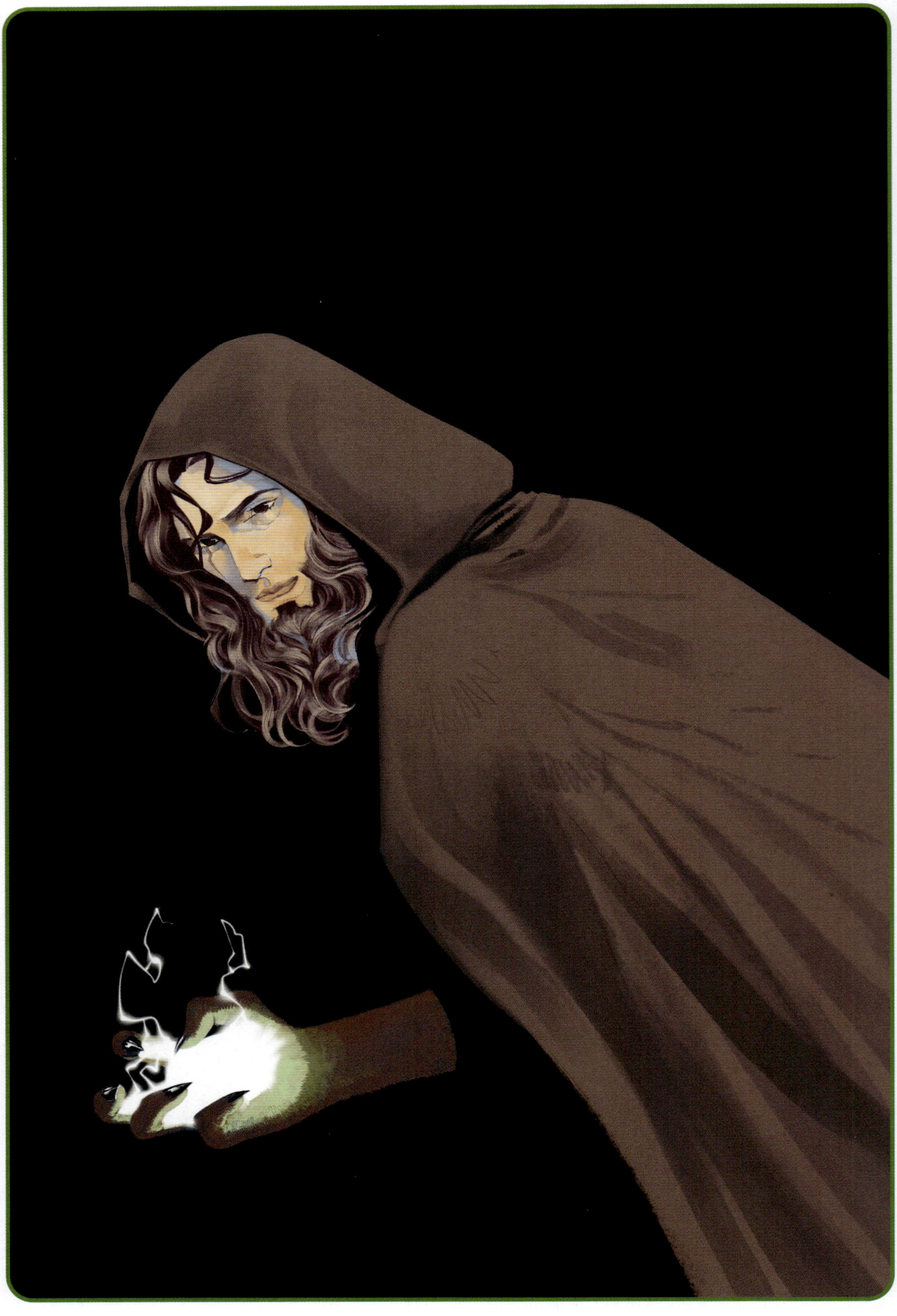

#3 VARIANT COVER
BY **HELENA MASELLIS**

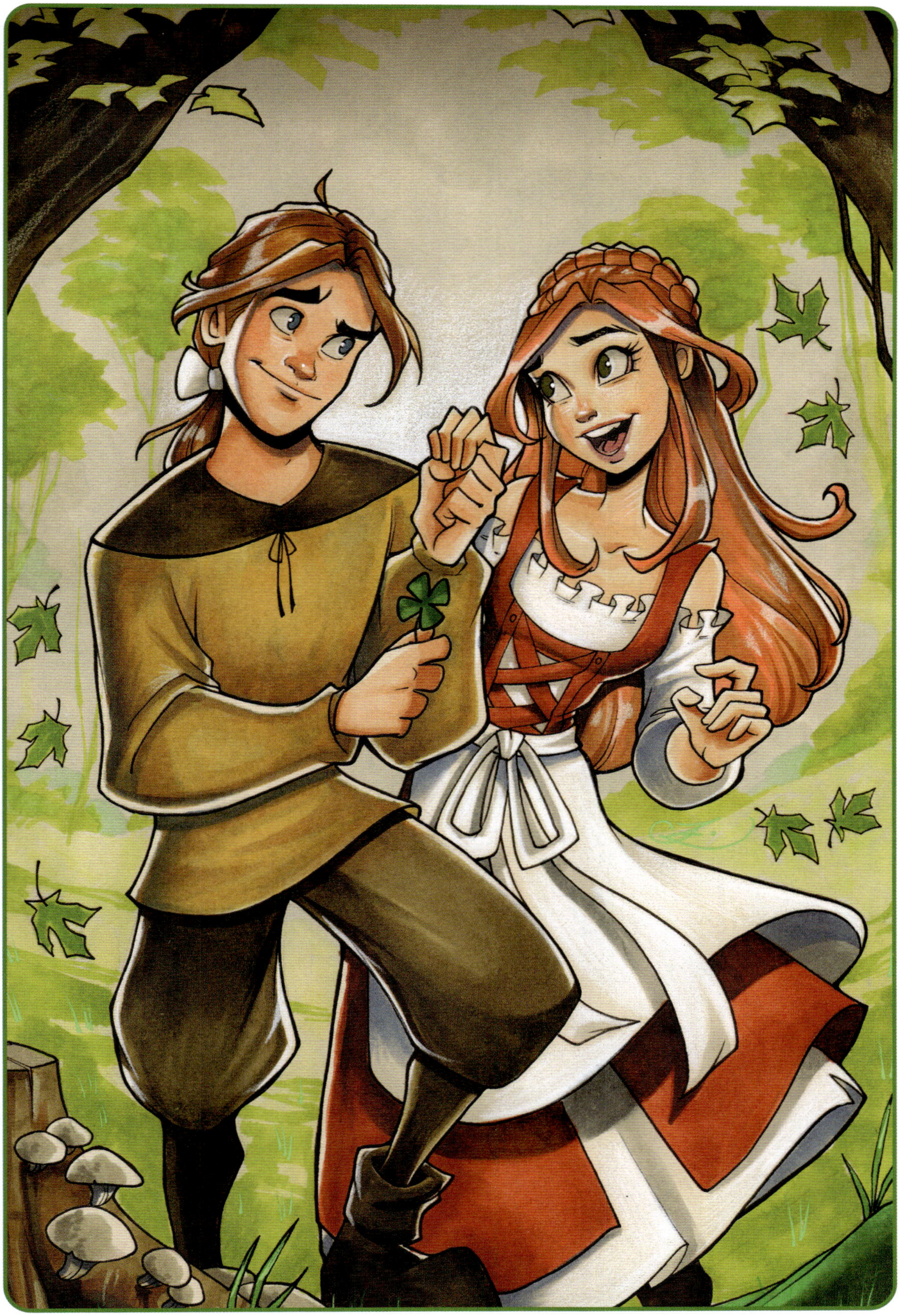

#4 VARIANT COVER
BY **CHRISSIE ZULLO**

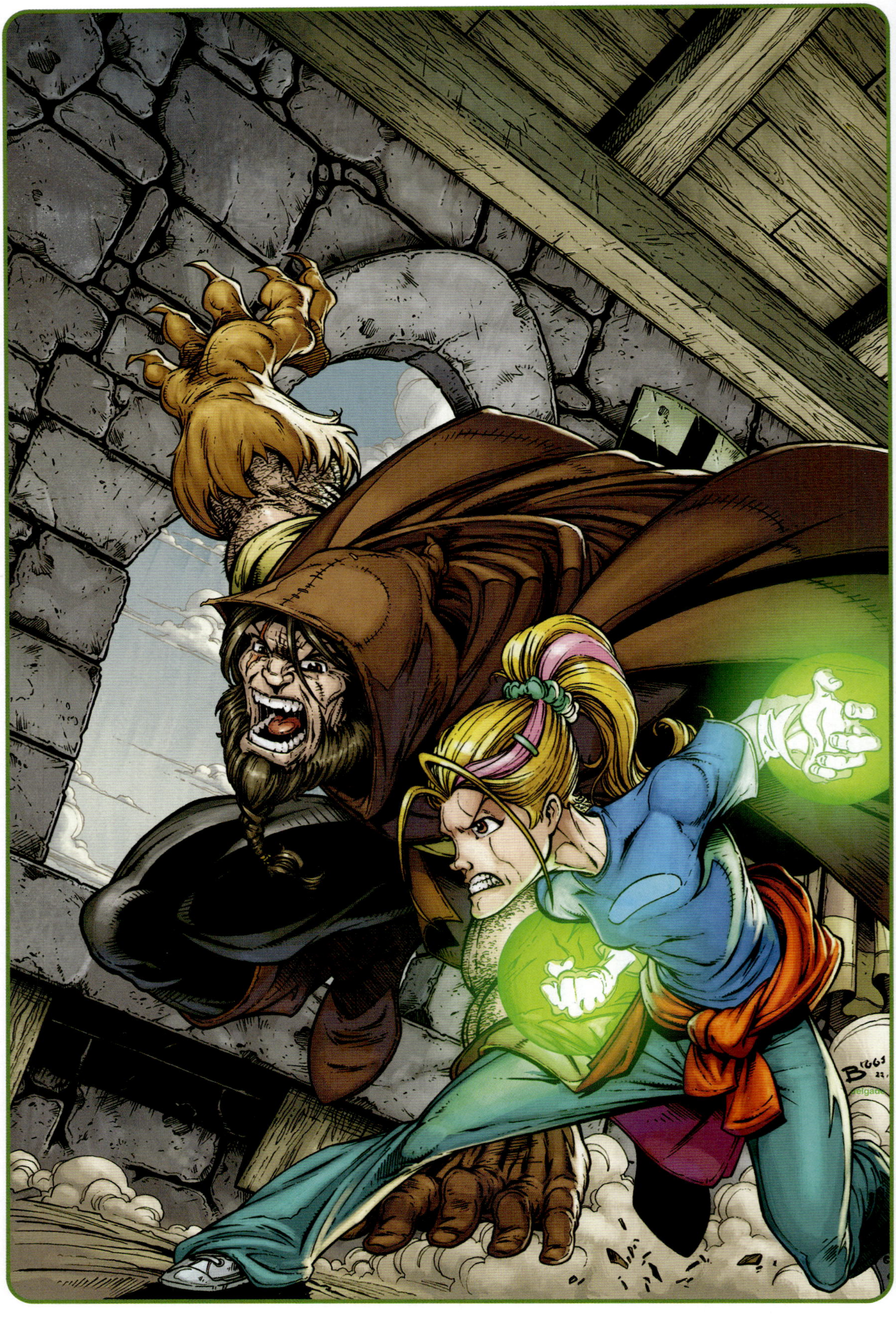

#4 VARIANT COVER
BY **JAMIE BIGGS**